WITHIN REACH: *Ten Stories*

WITHIN REACH

Ten Stories

Edited by
Donald R. Gallo

HarperCollins*Publishers*

WITHIN REACH
Ten Stories
For information address HarperCollins Children's Books,
a division of HarperCollins Publishers,
10 East 53rd Street, New York, NY 10022.

Library of Congress Cataloging-in-Publication Data
Within reach : ten stories / edited by Donald R. Gallo.
    p.   cm.
Summary: A collection of ten stories in which characters face choices,
risks, and challenges in their lives, by authors such as Constance C. Greene,
Judie Angell, and Robert Lipsyte.
    ISBN 0-06-021440-6. — ISBN 0-06-021441-4 (lib. bdg.)
    1. Children's stories, American.   [1. Short stories.]   I. Gallo, Donald R.
PZ5.W7566   1993   92-29378
[Fic]—dc20   CIP
                                                                           AC

Typography by Elynn Cohen
1   2   3   4   5   6   7   8   9   10
❖
First Edition

—for C.K. and her children

CONTENTS

INTRODUCTION   ix

POSSIBILITIES   1

Saturdays Is Peppermint   3
  by Constance C. Greene

The Secret Among the Stones   21
  by Ardath Mayhar

LAFFF   33
  by Lensey Namioka

NO GUARANTEES   51

I Saw What I Saw   53
  by Judie Angell

The Best Bedroom in Brooklyn   70
  by Carol Snyder

A Foolproof Plan   83
   by Steven Otfinoski

TAKING RISKS   95

A Brother's Promise   97
   by Pam Conrad

Futures File   117
   by Robert Lipsyte

Willie and the Christmas Spruce   129
   by Larry Bograd

Taking a Chance   152
   by Jan Greenberg

ABOUT THE EDITOR   179

INTRODUCTION

O ne of the hardest things about growing up is trying to be an individual. Standing on your own. You have to make choices, sometimes difficult ones. It's not just whether you choose red M&M's over brown ones, but whether you choose the right friends, say the right things, do something that others are not likely to do.

Making choices usually means taking risks. Reaching out to other people. Opening yourself to possible criticism or ridicule. Letting others see a part of you that they have never seen before. Being different from the rest of the group sometimes. But success is within reach.

In this book are ten stories about kids who take

risks, try new things, reach out to others. Sometimes they encounter challenges unexpectedly. Other times they seek out different paths for themselves. What are their chances of success? There are, of course, no guarantees when you try something different. But there are always hopeful possibilities.

These stories provide you with opportunities for new experiences, unexpected encounters. What are your chances for enjoying all of them? Well, there are no guarantees. Just hopeful possibilities. So: Make a choice. Pick a title that attracts you and jump right in. Or start from the beginning. Take a chance. Enjoyment is within reach.

WITHIN REACH: *Ten Stories*

POSSIBILITIES

SATURDAYS
IS PEPPERMINT

by Constance C. Greene

◆

The kid was really young; five, maybe, or at the max, six. I watched her from the corner of my eye as she battled tears. Her scruffy white tights wrinkled like crazy around her knobby knees and skinny ankles, like mine used to do. I wanted to lean across the aisle and tell her it would be all right, that the flight would be a piece of cake. No lightning, no thunder or turbulence. I remembered how I'd felt the first time I flew alone. All I could think of then was what I'd do if I got there in one piece and there was no one there to meet me.

She made passes at her mouth with her thumb. I could tell she was dying for a fix. But she didn't want to give in. I saw her tuck her grungy little blanket into her shoulder, where it would act as a

3

shield when the thumb finally made its way into her mouth.

I knew all the moves.

The flight attendant came down the aisle. I'd flown with her before. Her name was Zembra. She was a Mormon. I like to collect people of all different races and religions. Zembra was my first Mormon.

"Hi," I said as she paused to check if my seat belt was fastened and if my seat was in an upright position.

"Hey." I saw her draw a blank. Then she kicked in and said, "How are you anyway? Penny with a *y*, right? Off to Chicago to see your dad again?"

I was pleased she'd remembered my name. She must meet a heck of a lot of people every day. She was nice. She really liked kids. I can always tell. They don't all like kids, believe me. They fake it a lot, but they can't fool me.

"Yeah," I said. "He's got a new baby. A boy. My father's over the moon. He always wanted a son."

"So." Zembra's eyes roamed as she spoke. "That's good news. You've got a little brother. Terrific. What's his name?"

"Junior. What else? William Junior. Anne, that's my stepmother, she wanted to call him George after her father, but my father said he had to be Junior. He weighed eight pounds, two ounces. My father says he looks like an old boxing glove. He said I looked like an old boxing glove too. He says he wouldn't give a plugged nickel for any baby that didn't look like an old boxing glove."

"Yeah, but you improved a lot," Zembra said, grinning at me. "Your hair's gorgeous. I wish I had hair that color. Isn't her hair gorgeous?" Zembra asked the little kid, who pretended she wasn't listening to us.

Zembra opened the overhead compartment and got down two little pillows and some blankets for us.

"Anything you want to put up here, sweetie?" Zembra asked us both.

"No thanks," I said. "I'm all set." My carry-on bag was stowed under the seat.

"Lots of empty seats today," I said, like an old pro.

"When we take off, you can stretch out if you want," Zembra said. "Why don't you two girls sit together? You could keep each other company. How about it?"

"Sure," I said. "That'd be nice."

The little girl blinked and put her thumb in her mouth in a sort of defiant way, as if to say "I'm doing it and if you don't like it, tough."

I slipped into the seat next to her, and Zembra

touched my hair lightly. "I always wanted to be a redhead, on account of redheads have all the fun."

"I thought that was blondes," I said, blushing. People always tell me my hair is beautiful. They never mention the freckles. Or the nose. My nose is my cross that I have to bear. But maybe not forever. If we can afford it, I might get a nose job when I'm sixteen. My mother has a new boyfriend who's a plastic surgeon. She really likes him. She said maybe he'll give us a discount on a nose job if their relationship turns into anything.

In the meantime, my hair's my crowning glory. My only glory, if you want the truth. If I ever lost my hair, they might lash me to an ice floe and shove me out to sea.

I'm thirteen and holding, waiting for a miracle so when I wake up and look in the mirror, my beauty will take my breath away.

"What's your name, sweetie?" Zembra asked the kid, who hooked her index finger over her nose and sucked on her thumb noisily and didn't answer.

"Hey, we're all friends here," Zembra said. "Everything's nice and cozy, and after takeoff I'll bring around the drinks cart; then we'll serve you one of our delicious lunches. You'll go crazy for this one. Chicken and peas and our special chocolate delight. Yum." Zembra crossed her eyes and rubbed her stomach.

The kid broke up. She giggled until she ran out of steam.

Zembra smiled, pleased. "See there," she said. "Good for you. What's your name, now?"

"Eliza," the little girl said.

"Oho, like the girl who crossed the ice in *Uncle Tom's Cabin*," Zembra said as she walked away. "I hated that book. We had to read it in eighth grade, I remember."

"That's the grade I'm in," I said.

"You must be in junior high," Eliza said, staring at me. "Jennifer's in ninth grade. She's my baby-sitter. Jennifer doesn't go out on dates yet. I love her. We play dominoes and slapjack and she lets me try on her jewelry. She's got a ring made of real gold." Eliza's big eyes got even bigger. "And all these bracelets." Her voice and her face went all dreamy, contemplating Jennifer's bracelets.

"My mother's buying me a gold locket with a place to put her picture in when I stop sucking my thumb," Eliza told me. "Do you like jewelry?"

"It's okay," I said. I'd really rather have a horse.

"My mother's on her honeymoon, you see." Eliza had decided to open up. "I wanted to go too, but they said it was too expensive. To fly to Hawaii, that is. That's where people go on their honeymoon. It's a long way away. I'm going to stay with my aunt. She's got two boys and they're monsters. They're wild. Only I'm not supposed to say anything because my aunt's taking care of me and she's doing us a big favor. I'm bringing her a present. Want to see?"

"Sure," I said.

Eliza rummaged through her backpack and brought out a box of dusting powder. "Smell," she said, sticking it under my nose.

"Um. Very delicious," I said. "It smells like cotton candy."

"If you ask me, it smells pink. My aunt will like it, though, because she doesn't have money for many luxuries."

"You talk very grown-up," I said. "How old are you anyway?"

"I'm five and three quarters. Do you have a mother?" Eliza asked.

"Everybody has a mother," I said.

"No they don't. I have two friends and they don't have a mother, they only have a father. My father died when his motorcycle crashed," she told me. "That was before I was even born. So I never even *knew* my father." She lifted her hands, palms up, and shrugged so her shoulders almost touched her ears. "So now my mother and my new father are on their honeymoon. He doesn't really like children." Her eyes were very bright blue. They glittered at me. "My mother says if I'm very good and don't make a lot of noise or anything, he'll get to like me. We discussed it, and we decided I should call him Dad. So I'm calling him Dad."

"That sounds good," I said.

The plane dropped and bounced around in the sky as if it were on a trampoline. Eliza reached out and took my hand. I could feel my stomach churning.

"Want me to tell your fortune?" I asked.

Zembra came down the aisle, touching each seat as she went to steady herself. "How're you two doing?" she said.

"Okay," I said. "I'm telling her fortune."

"Good for you." And Zembra continued on down the aisle.

The pilot came on and said we were experiencing some turbulence and he'd try to fly above it.

"Miss," I heard a querulous voice say. "I'm feeling unwell. My son's waiting for me at the airport. I do hope the flight will be on time. If the flight's not on time, he might not wait for me."

Zembra's voice, calm and easy, said everything was fine, just fine.

I squinted down at Eliza's palm. At school, we tell a lot of fortunes, mostly about how many boys will love us, how rich we'll be. Basic stuff.

"Your lifeline is very strong," I said, tracing her lifeline with my finger.

"That tickles," she said, giggling.

"I see two, no, three kids, all girls. I see that very soon you are going to stop sucking your thumb. You will have a very happy life with your mother and your new father, who will love you very much. You will have lots of good times and they will be very proud of you."

Eliza took a few swipes at her mouth with her thumb but didn't put it in.

"Did you know I have underpants with the days of the week on them?" she said. "Tuesdays is blue and Wednesdays is orange and Fridays is purple. That way I don't get mixed up."

"Good for you," I said. "Did you know I sucked my thumb until I was eleven?" I don't know what made me tell her that. It just slipped out.

"Eleven!" She was shocked. "That's awful old to still suck your thumb."

"Yeah, and right after I stopped, I got sick and had to stay in bed for a week. Boy, I wanted to suck that old thumb in the worst way." I rolled my eyes at her. "You know how it is—when you're sad or lonely or tired, the thumb really helps."

Eliza nodded.

"Does yours taste different on different days of the week, like that medicine that Mary Poppins pours out?" I asked her.

Again she nodded. "Some days it's strawberry," she said softly, "and some days it's sort of vanilla."

The plane shuddered suddenly, as if someone had walked over its grave.

"Saturdays is peppermint," Eliza said.

"What is?" I said through clenched teeth.

"Well, my thumb. What else? We're talking about how it tastes different on different days. Kind of like my underpants," Eliza said solemnly. "On Saturdays, it's always peppermint."

I thought about that. It sort of made sense. The plane was doing fine now. Eliza leaned close and said, "I have to go to the bathroom. Will you come with me? I never went to the bathroom on an airplane before."

"Follow me," I said. We unbuckled ourselves and wobbled down the aisle. There was no line at the toilets. Both of them were empty.

"Just go in and sit down, same as on the ground," I said. "Don't lock the door. I'll be right here. There isn't room inside for both of us. If you need help, holler."

She left the bathroom door open a crack. When she came out, she looked proud of herself.

"I would like to ask you something," she said when we got back to our seats. "Is it all right if I whisper?"

I bent down so she could reach my ear.

"Where does it go when you go to the bathroom in an airplane?" she whispered.

I laughed, but only a little. I had wondered the same thing my first time. "They have a giant container that catches it, and when they clean the plane, they empty the container."

"Oh." She seemed relieved. "I thought maybe it just flew through the air and hit people on the ground on the head. Like sometimes when you're driving along and a bird goes to the bathroom and it hits the windshield. Once a bird went to the bathroom on my head and it was all yucky." She pulled a long face.

"I'm glad it's not like that," she said. "I wouldn't like it if a real person did that to me."

Zembra came by with the drinks cart. I had a ginger ale and Eliza had a Coke. Then we had lunch. Zembra put the trays on the little table and said, "Well, nice to see you girls are turning out to be good buddies. Maybe you could be pen pals too. Here's your chicken and peas and chocolate delight. Just the way I told you. Don't say I never gave you anything. *Bon appétit.*"

Eliza cleaned her plate. Then she took the little packets of salt and pepper and sugar and salad dressing and stuffed them into her backpack.

"I would take this too." She held up the tiny container of half-and-half they give you for tea or coffee. "But it might spill, so I better leave it."

She really was too much. I wanted to hug her hard, but she might not like being hugged. Not everyone likes it. How could that creepola her mother was on her honeymoon with not like this kid? I wouldn't have minded taking her home with me. She could be my little sister. I would like a little sister. Let's face it, my little brother wasn't going to be much good to me. For one thing, he was a lot younger, and another, we weren't going to live in the same house. I'd only see him a couple times a year. Then, just when we started getting used to each other, and started playing and fooling around, I'd have to leave and go back home. Maybe if I asked, my mother would let me bring him home with me when he got old enough to travel without diapers. He wasn't *her* little boy, but he was my brother, after all. But maybe my mother wouldn't even *like* my little brother.

After lunch we played cards. Eliza had this game where the one who got all reds first won. She had made it up, she said. She liked to shuffle and deal. She won every time.

"Lucky we're not playing for money," I said. "I'd be broke."

"At home, me and my friends play for chips," she said. "Each chip is worth about a billion dollars.

Like at Vegas. My mother went there and she was going to take me, only they told her they don't allow children there. What kind of a place doesn't allow children, anyway, I'd like to know?" Eliza said indignantly.

"Maybe it's against the law, on account of all the gambling," I said.

"I would like to go to Disney World," Eliza said, shuffling the cards in a professional way. "My friend Jamie sent me a postcard from Disney World and it had a big picture of Mickey and Minnie on the front. Jamie said it was the most fun in the world."

Zembra came to take our trays away, and Eliza said, "Thank you for the good lunch."

"Well, that's a first," Zembra said, laughing. "Usually they tell me how lousy it was. You're a couple of nice kids, if you ask me. If I could, I'd put you both in my pocket and take you home with me."

"Do you have any children?" Eliza said.

"Nope. No chick nor child nor husband," Zembra said. "Not even a dog. All I've got is a VCR and a beat-up Chevy."

"How old are you?" Eliza asked.

"Thirty-seven," Zembra replied, not batting an eye. "And I'm not thrilled about it, but there it is. Still in my prime, though."

"My mother's almost forty," Eliza said. "She'll be forty her next birthday. She says she's still a kid, though. She wants somebody to take care of her. I said I'd take care of her, but she said she meant a husband. So now she's got one."

We were quiet, digesting this information.

"I know a dirty word," Eliza said. "Want to hear it?"

"Uh-oh," Zembra said. "I'm not sure I'm up to this."

"Shot!" Eliza said, hissing the word through her teeth. Then she put her hands over her eyes, fingers splayed, and peered out at us, waiting for our reaction.

"Well, if that doesn't beat all," said Zembra, shaking her head and winking at me.

"Wow. So that's the dirty word, huh?" I said.

Eliza nodded vigorously. "Shot! Shot! Shot!" She fired off a rapid volley of shots. I could tell she liked the feel of the dirty word rolling around in her mouth.

"A boy in school told me I better not say that word in front of my mother or she'd wash out my mouth with soap," Eliza said. "But he doesn't know my mother."

"That's one I missed," I said.

"Live and learn," Zembra said, stacking the trays.

"Miss! Miss!" came the querulous voice from the rear. "Would you come here for a moment, please?"

We had time for one more card game. Then the seat-belt sign came on and the pilot said we were preparing for a landing. And to please stay seated until the aircraft came to a full stop.

"Maybe we could write each other a letter," Eliza said, holding her thumb close to her mouth and looking longingly at it.

"That'd be good," I said.

"Of course, I'm not too good of a writer," she said, "but my mother would help me."

I wrote my name and address on a paper napkin and gave it to her.

She stuffed it into her backpack. In large, uneven letters she wrote ELIZA BENNETT on another paper napkin.

"I live on Cedar Street," she told me. "You know where Cedar Street is?"

"What town are we talking about here?" I asked.

She frowned. "It's in New Jersey," she said.

"That's the state. What town do you live in?"

"Oh, town. That's Somerville. I go to school there too. My telephone number is . . ." She fluttered her eyelashes and thumped the seat in front of her with her feet.

"That's okay. I can look it up," I said. "We can be pen pals, sort of. Like Zembra said. I'll write you a letter and you can write me back. How would that be?"

"Probably we can be friends forevermore," Eliza said wistfully. "Like in a book."

"I'll miss you," I told her.

It was true. How can you miss someone you've only known for a few hours? I wondered.

I tucked the paper napkin with Eliza's name and address on it into my pocket carefully, so I wouldn't lose it.

As the plane taxied to the gate, we gathered up our gear.

"You girls all set?" Zembra asked. "Spence will meet you outside and escort Eliza to her aunt, see she's taken care of."

"I want *you* to escort me," Eliza said, tugging at me.

"Spence is an okay dude," I said. "First time I flew alone, he took me out to meet my father. Don't get bent out of shape, kid. I'll come with you. No sweat."

Zembra patted Eliza's head. "Good-bye, sweetie," she said. "Take care."

"See you, Zem," I said, keeping it light for everybody's sake.

Eliza and I were the last ones off. Spence was

waiting, biting his fingernails. Spence is a very nervous person. He's into white-water rafting and coin collecting.

"Yo," Spence said. He always says "Yo." Spence has thin hair. "Who wants fat hair?" Spence says. He can be quite funny at times.

The three of us walked down the corridor and out into the terminal.

"There she is!" A woman in a red coat waved both arms. "Here, Eliza! Over here!"

Eliza took off like a shot. She didn't look back. I saw the woman scoop her up in a bear hug. The two little boys with her danced around in a circle, showing off. Eliza would be all right.

"There's my father," I told Spence. He touched his finger to his forehead and said "Yo," then split.

My father loped toward me across the vast expanse of polished floor. He had one of those baby carriers strapped to his chest. I ran, my bag thumping against my side.

"Hi, Dad," I said. I'm always a little awkward when we first meet. So is he.

"So you made it," he said, smiling, patting the bulge inside the baby carrier. He always says that when he meets me. So you made it.

"Here he is." And my father, with an expression on his face I'd never seen before, pulled back the blue blanket. I peeked in. All I could see was a bald head and an ancient, mushed-up face.

"You're right, Dad," I said. "He *does* look like an old boxing glove." It was just something to say. I wanted to make my father laugh.

Instead, I was dismayed and flabbergasted to see his eyes fill with sudden tears.

"Oh, Dad," I said. "He's beautiful."

My father smiled. "So are you, darling," he said. He put his free arm around me. I moved closer. My face was on a level with his.

"You've grown," he said with some surprise. "You're taller than you were last time."

He was right. Before, we'd walked easily, arms around each other, taking long steps. Now and then I'd lay my head on his shoulder. Now I didn't fit. I squeezed up my eyes and bent my knees, just a fraction, and kept pace with my father and my little brother.

As we worked our way out to the parking lot, I wondered if I'd tell him about Eliza. I knew he'd get a kick out of hearing the dirty-word story.

If the right moment came, I decided, I would tell him about her. But I might not.

If I kept her packed away in a little compartment in my head, maybe she'd last longer. I'd have to see.

ABOUT THIS STORY

Because of the high rate of divorce, young children often have to travel alone on airplanes to visit parents in distant locations. After reading a newspaper article containing airline statistics about these children, Constance Greene began to think about the loneliness a young traveler might feel. In real life, some children are in tears the entire trip. Others make friends who help them through the worst, she learned. "This story started out to be a humorous one," Ms. Greene says, "but it turned into a poignant one instead."

ABOUT THE AUTHOR

Constance C. Greene loves to observe children and eavesdrop on their conversations, then write about them. She got her training for that first from working with the Associated Press and then from having her own children and, more recently, grandchildren. Her mother, father, and grandfather were all newspaper people. Her most popular books for middle-school readers are *Beat the Turtle Drum* and *A Girl Called Al.* The success of that first book about Al resulted in a series of five more books, the most recent of which is *Al's Blind Date.* Ms. Greene is also the author of *The Love Letters of J. Timothy Owens,* and has just published *Odds on Oliver,* a funny book that describes the adventures of Oliver as he tries to be a hero.

THE SECRET AMONG THE STONES

by Ardath Mayhar

The sun was blisteringly hot. Caro pulled her hat down over her ears as a gritty gust threatened to send it flying away down the steep canyon below her perch.

The climb had been hard and dusty. She was exhausted, and she hated wearing a hat, but sitting on this gritty boulder in the desert sun without one would have been crazy.

She was almost at the top of the mesa now, the steep trail behind her leading down into shadow, for the sun was slanting toward the west already. All around was the vast expanse of broken land, flatlands shimmering with heat-haze, flat-topped mesas rising in the distance, scrub showing its dusty green wherever there was a trace or the hope of water.

The others in her class had gone ahead, led by Miss Burke, who never seemed to be troubled by heat or dust or stones in her shoes. Caro could hear the babble of their voices, but once she had the pebble out of her Nike she hated to move.

There was nothing she wanted to see up there on the tableland. Ruins, as far as she was concerned, were nothing but tumbles of rocks. She had no interest in the ancient people who had cut the stones and set them in place.

She took a sip from her canteen, thinking wryly how silly she'd thought it when Miss Burke insisted that every member of the class must have one, filled, before the bus left the motel.

The shadows beneath the height were inky in contrast to the bone-pale glare of the sun. She gazed into the depths, resting her eyes, and edges and curves came into focus.

That looked like a fascinating place down there, Caro thought. Instead of going up, which was going to be hot and tiring, she decided to go down again and cut back into the shade of the canyon. The last member of the class had already gone by, and nobody could make an objection.

Caro tied her scarf over her hat to help hold it on, made sure that her Nikes were free of pebbles, and started down. Miss Burke was entirely too far away now to notice one of her sheep going astray.

The guide was leading the group. By the time anyone realized she was gone, the class would be back down on a level with her destination.

The way down was surprisingly difficult, because it was hard to see the footing. Miss Burke had cautioned everyone about walking carefully, and now Caro saw why. A misstep could send her tumbling down the steep path to splatter on the rocks below.

She felt her way cautiously, watching her feet, freezing when she heard a slithery sound that might be a snake. It turned out to be a dust-colored lizard, but she found her heart thudding hard and hot liquid rising in her throat. What if it *had* been a rattlesnake? She shivered and went even more slowly.

At the bottom of the slope the raw-edged cut, which her party had ignored before, led into a walled space opening out into a wider area. The sandy grit of the floor was swept into riffles by the wind pulled through the corridor in the rock; she had a strange feeling that no human being had ever set foot there.

Now that she was out of the sun, Caro's eyes adjusted to the dimness. Someone had been here after all. There were markings on the walls, random doodlings as if someone had occupied him- or herself by drawing circles and jagged lines of lightning and stick figures. She went close and stared up at the pictures, which must have been drawn by someone much taller than she.

There was a story there, she thought, running her gaze along the wall of the canyon. There had been a terrible rain—the slanting dashes couldn't be anything else. Then the sun had cooked everything, for she could see horned shapes that had to be the skulls of buffalo and crosshatched marks that might mean the ground had cracked with drought. There were sketchy shapes of buffalo and deer and men holding sticks and bows.

Interesting. Caro was glad she had stopped and let the others go on without her. She had seen many pictures of the ruins on top of the mesa, but she'd never seen anything about this slot of canyon with drawings on its walls.

She moved back and forth across the space, checking for further markings, but there were no more. Instead, she saw a cave cut back into the eastern wall, its entrance so low that even she would have to stoop and crawl to get inside. A good place for snakes, Caro suspected, but even so she bent to stare into the dark recess.

There was something inside. A bundle of cloth? A stick? Something else, hard to see in the depths where it lay.

Score another for Miss Burke. She had dictated

the contents of each hiker's pack, and there had to be a small flashlight and spare batteries. Caro had considered it silly, carrying all this stuff for miles up and down desert heights, but now she had a light.

She thumbed the button, and the narrow beam flicked into the little cave. She gave a stifled shriek and fell back to sit in the grit, staring at the thing that looked back at her from hollow eye sockets. She was almost eye to eye with a skull.

Feeling a chill of terror, Caro shivered, but she didn't retreat. Now she could see that the bundle was clothing of some kind. The stick was a leg bone, which she recognized only because they had studied bones in science last month.

The skull was small, not any larger than her own, she thought. Wisps of black hair straggled from its crown, and it lay on the dusty remnants of a long braid. Even a fragment of a feather still clung to the strands.

Caro had a sudden feeling that this had been a girl, just like herself. Had she been trapped here and starved to death? The entry into the canyon looked raw, as if it had recently been cracked open by some shifting of the rock. Could it have been another such shift that caught this one here?

But surely there was another end to the canyon. . . . She scrambled upright and ran to see. The space ended after a dozen winding yards at a wall of rock that went up and up, as smoothly as if it had been sliced with a knife. There wasn't a handhold to be seen. Suddenly sure that she was right—the girl had been trapped—Caro returned to the cave and sat down on a flat stone to stare, fascinated and repelled, at her find.

This was a well-known area in a national park. Surely the archeologists had known about this place for years and had studied those markings and measured this pitiful remnant of humanity. Yet if that were so, why hadn't they removed it to a museum or something? It didn't make much sense.

The canyon was warmer than she had expected, and Caro took off her hat and fanned herself as she sat in the shadow of the cliff, trying to decide what to do. The skull gazed with mournful intensity into the beam of her flash. The teeth were small, even, not jagged and stained like those of the museum skulls. This had to be a child about her own age, twelve or so.

Caro searched the interior of the space with her light, but she could see no movement that might be a snake. No scorpion sidled out of range. She felt compelled, though she had no idea why, to venture in and sort out this discovery.

"I am not brave," she said, marveling at the impulse. "I can't stand spiders or blood or anything my brothers like. But I have got to see what's in there. This is *mine!*"

Laying aside her hat, she went down on hands and knees, holding the flash in her teeth. She moved into the cramped space. It was low and dry, and smelled of dust and something very, very old. Not a dead smell, but a snuffy, acrid one.

When she was within a few feet of the pitiful little body, she stopped and looked at it, holding herself still with an effort. Behind the bundle of clothing was another leg bone, bent at the knee. A fall of finger bones extended from beneath a flap of leather sleeve, and something bright—beads?— decorated the upper part of the garment.

Caro knew better than to touch anything, but she felt it couldn't hurt to see it all, now that she had begun. She crawled forward and peered into the shadow behind the bundle of clothing. A small shape lay beside the other skeletal hand.

This was easily identified: a doll, made of a stick, with some sort of fur for hair and a leather dress. Two stick legs extended from beneath the dusty skirt.

Caro breathed a long sigh and settled onto the floor of the cave, knowing she had been right. She closed her eyes and saw, as if she were there, a little girl dressed in leather, playing in this shady place with her doll.

The vision seemed true and real, and she clicked off the flashlight, gazing into that distant past. The child was singing softly, a sort of chant, as she rocked the doll in her arms.

"Ai-hi-yee! Ai-hi-yee!" echoed in Caro's mind.

This was a secret place, Caro thought, forgotten by the child's elders, though the markings on the walls showed that others had known it. She came here, as Caro often went to her own secret place beyond the rock formation at home, to think, to dream, to sing to her doll.

As Caro watched that vision, the dream-sky darkened, making the canyon go black as night. Lightning scarred the upper air, its flash brightening the canyon in short bursts. There came a terrific blast of sound, followed by a rumble and a roar.

Terror filled her, and Caro opened her eyes and clicked on the flashlight again. The little shape lay still, its shadow harsh behind it, and Caro knew she had dreamed truly. This child had been trapped here by a rockslide caused, perhaps, by a lightning strike; no one among her people had known where to search for her.

"Did you starve to death?" She shivered. "Were you even more afraid than I was, just now?" Caro murmured, bending forward to lay a comforting hand on the leather sleeve.

Where she touched it, the ancient material powdered away to dust, leaving the slender arm bones exposed. Caro sighed. No, she mustn't touch anything else. She had to get Miss Burke, even if it meant climbing to the top of the mesa to report this discovery.

She felt sure the most recent storm, with the landslips and rockslides it had set off a few weeks back, must have opened the way that an ancient catastrophe had closed. There had been something on the news about an earth tremor caused by water going down into crevices in the mesas.

She backed out and retrieved her hat. Then Caro hurried to find her teacher, who knew what to do about everything. She met the group coming down the mesa, calling her name anxiously and searching every crevice into which she might have fallen.

"Oh, Miss Burke! I'm not lost, just out of pocket. I've found something awful and wonderful!" she panted.

"Carolyn, I cannot have my charges running off in country like this! It's dangerous. . . . *What* have you found?" Miss Burke was an amateur archeologist, and any hint of ancient finds caught her attention instantly.

By the time she saw the newly opened way into the canyon and the small bones in the cave, Miss Burke was as excited as she ever allowed herself to become. "I will inform the Rangers as soon as we get back to the motel," she said, her gaze fixed longingly on the half-visible bundle beneath the cliff.

She turned to José, who had been the guide for this field trip. "It will surprise me if this is not extremely unusual. Not because of the skeleton, of course, but because of the petroglyphs."

He stared into the cave, still looking astonished. "I think maybe you are right," he said. "We will call the University when we have the chance."

Caro felt sure this was something really important. She had a vision of returning in triumph to the scene of her discovery. The Carolyn Wheaton Canyon Area had a nice ring to it. She had a sudden vision of her triumph, lights, reporters, awed schoolmates and teachers.

Then she thought of that dark cave where the small skeleton still lay, heard again in her memory the devastating thunder, felt again the cold despair that had touched her as she crouched in that place.

There was tragedy here, not triumph. The fame that might come of it was not hers at all.

"Ai-hi-yee!" she whispered, as she bent to look through the dimness into those empty eyes once more. "Ai-hi-yee!"

The small, even teeth grinned at her silently.

Caro smiled back. She had done her best for this lost one. Maybe—who could say?—this girl knew at last that she was no longer alone.

ABOUT THIS STORY

"The Secret Among the Stones" grew out of the research that Ardath Mayhar did for a novel about the cliff dwellers on Mesa Verde in Colorado. "Having for years been interested in the Anasazi," she says, "I found that the deeper I dug, the greater my fascination became. This small story used only one tiny fragment of the rich tapestry that is our West."

ABOUT THE AUTHOR

In addition to writing Western novels for adults under the pseudonym Frank Cannon, Ardath Mayhar has raised broiler chickens, owned and operated a bookstore, and at various times been a dairy farmer, a postal clerk, a proofreader, and a teacher. More often than not, though, she has been a writer of science fiction and fantasy, and has even written long dramatic narrative verses in those genres. About one fourth of her publications have been for middle-grade readers, with *Medicine Walk* and *Carrots and Miggle* her most popular books. Her most recent novels are *A Place for Silver Silence*—a science-fiction story for young adults—and *The People of the Mesa*, a historical novel about the cliff dwellers described in part in "The Secret Among the Stones."

LAFFF

by Lensey Namioka

In movies, geniuses have frizzy white hair, right? They wear thick glasses and have names like Dr. Zweistein.

Peter Lu didn't have frizzy white hair. He had straight hair, as black as licorice. He didn't wear thick glasses, either, since his vision was normal.

Peter's family, like ours, had immigrated from China, but they had settled here first. When we moved into a house just two doors down from the Lus, they gave us some good advice on how to get along in America.

I went to the same school as Peter, and we walked to the school bus together every morning. Like many Chinese parents, mine made sure that I worked very hard in school.

In spite of all I could do, my grades were nothing compared to Peter's. He was at the top in all his classes. We walked to the school bus without talking because I was a little scared of him. Besides, he was always deep in thought.

Peter didn't have any friends. Most of the kids thought he was a nerd because they saw his head always buried in books. I didn't think he even tried to join the rest of us or cared what the others thought of him.

Then on Halloween he surprised us all. As I went down the block trick-or-treating, dressed as a zucchini in my green sweats, I heard a strange, deep voice behind me say, "How do you do."

I yelped and turned around. Peter was wearing a long, black Chinese gown with slits in the sides. On his head he had a little round cap, and down each side of his mouth drooped a thin, long mustache.

"I am Dr. Lu Manchu, the mad scientist," he announced, putting his hands in his sleeves and bowing.

He smiled when he saw me staring at his costume. It was a scary smile, somehow.

Some of the other kids came up, and when they saw Peter, they were impressed. "Hey, neat!" said one boy.

I hadn't expected Peter to put on a costume

and go trick-or-treating like a normal kid. So maybe he did want to join the others after all—at least some of the time. After that night he wasn't a nerd anymore. He was Dr. Lu Manchu. Even some of the teachers began to call him that.

When we became too old for trick-or-treating, Peter was still Dr. Lu Manchu. The rumor was that he was working on a fantastic machine in his parents' garage. But nobody had any idea what it was.

One evening, as I was coming home from a baby-sitting job, I cut across the Lus' backyard. Passing their garage, I saw through a little window that the light was on. My curiosity got the better of me, and I peeked in.

I saw a booth that looked like a shower stall. A stool stood in the middle of the stall, and hanging over the stool was something that looked like a great big shower head.

Suddenly a deep voice behind me said, "Good evening, Angela." Peter bowed and smiled his scary smile. He didn't have his costume on and he didn't have the long, droopy mustache. But he was Dr. Lu Manchu.

"What are you doing?" I squeaked.

Still in his strange, deep voice, Peter said, "What are *you* doing? After all, this is my garage."

"I was just cutting across your yard to get

home. Your parents never complained before."

"I thought you were spying on me," said Peter. "I thought you wanted to know about my machine." He hissed when he said the word *machine*.

Honestly, he was beginning to frighten me. "What machine?" I demanded. "You mean this shower-stall thing?"

He drew himself up and narrowed his eyes, making them into thin slits. "This is my time machine!"

I goggled at him. "You mean . . . you mean . . . this machine can send you forward and backward in time?"

"Well, actually, I can only send things forward in time," admitted Peter, speaking in his normal voice again. "That's why I'm calling the machine LAFFF. It stands for Lu's Artifact For Fast Forward."

Of course Peter always won first prize at the annual statewide science fair. But that's a long way from making a time machine. Minus his mustache and long Chinese gown, he was just Peter Lu.

"I don't believe it!" I said. "I bet LAFFF is only good for a laugh."

"Okay, Angela. I'll show you!" hissed Peter.

He sat down on the stool and twisted a dial. I heard some *bleep*s, *cheep*s, and *gurgle*s. Peter disappeared.

He must have done it with mirrors. I looked around the garage. I peeked under the tool bench. There was no sign of him.

"Okay, I give up," I told him. "It's a good trick, Peter. You can come out now."

Bleep, *cheep*, and *gurgle* went the machine, and there was Peter, sitting on the stool. He held a red rose in his hand. "What do you think of that?"

I blinked. "So you produced a flower. Maybe you had it under the stool."

"Roses bloom in June, right?" he demanded.

That was true. And this was December.

"I sent myself forward in time to June when the flowers were blooming," said Peter. "And I picked the rose from our yard. Convinced, Angela?"

It was too hard to swallow. "You said you couldn't send things back in time," I objected. "So how did you bring the rose back?"

But even as I spoke I saw that his hands were empty. The rose was gone.

"That's one of the problems with the machine," said Peter. "When I send myself forward, I can't seem to stay there for long. I snap back to my own time after only a minute. Anything I bring with me snaps back to its own time, too. So my rose has gone back to this June."

I was finally convinced, and I began to see possibilities. "Wow, just think: If I don't want to do the dishes, I can send myself forward to the time when the dishes are already done."

"That won't do you much good," said Peter. "You'd soon pop back to the time when the dishes were still dirty."

Too bad. "There must be something your machine is good for," I said. Then I had another idea. "Hey, you can bring me back a piece of fudge from the future, and I can eat it twice: once now, and again in the future."

"Yes, but the fudge wouldn't stay in your stomach," said Peter. "It would go back to the future."

"That's even better!" I said. "I can enjoy eating the fudge over and over again without getting fat!"

It was late, and I had to go home before my parents started to worry. Before I left, Peter said, "Look, Angela, there's still a lot of work to do on LAFFF. Please don't tell anybody about the machine until I've got it right."

A few days later I asked him how he was doing.

"I can stay in the future time a bit longer now," he said. "Once I got it up to four minutes."

"Is that enough time to bring me back some fudge from the future?" I asked.

"We don't keep many sweets around the house," he said. "But I'll see what I can do."

A few minutes later, he came back with a spring roll for me. "My mother was frying these in the kitchen, and I snatched one while she wasn't looking."

I bit into the hot, crunchy spring roll, but before I finished chewing, it disappeared. The taste of soy sauce, green onions, and bean sprouts stayed a little longer in my mouth, though.

It was fun to play around with LAFFF, but it wasn't really useful. I didn't know what a great help it would turn out to be.

———

Every year our school held a writing contest, and the winning story for each grade got printed in our school magazine. I wanted desperately to win. I worked awfully hard in school, but my parents still thought I could do better.

Winning the writing contest would show my parents that I was really good in something. I love writing stories, and I have lots of ideas. But when I actually write them down, my stories never turn out as good as I thought. I just can't seem to find the right words, because English isn't my first language.

I got an honorable mention last year, but it wasn't the same as winning and showing my parents my name, Angela Tang, printed in the school magazine.

The deadline for the contest was getting close, and I had a pile of stories written, but none of them looked like a winner.

Then, the day before the deadline, *boing*, a brilliant idea hit me.

I thought of Peter and his LAFFF machine.

I rushed over to the Lus' garage and, just as I had hoped, Peter was there, tinkering with his machine.

"I've got this great idea for winning the story contest," I told him breathlessly. "You see, to be certain of winning, I have to write the story that would be the winner."

"That's obvious," Peter said dryly. "In fact, you're going around in a circle."

"Wait, listen!" I said. "I want to use LAFFF and go forward to the time when the next issue of the school magazine is out. Then I can read the winning story."

After a moment Peter nodded. "I see. You plan to write down the winning story after you've read it and then send it in to the contest."

I nodded eagerly. "The story would *have* to win, because it's the winner!"

Peter began to look interested. "I've got LAFFF to the point where I can stay in the future for seven minutes now. Will that be long enough for you?"

"I'll just have to work quickly," I said.

Peter smiled. It wasn't his scary Lu Manchu

smile, but a nice smile. He was getting as excited as I was. "Okay, Angela. Let's go for it."

He led me to the stool. "What's your destination?" he asked. "I mean, *when's* your destination?"

Suddenly I was nervous. I told myself that Peter had made many time trips, and he looked perfectly healthy.

Why not? What have I got to lose—except time?

I took a deep breath. "I want to go forward three weeks in time." By then I'd have a copy of the new school magazine in my room.

"Ready, Angela?" asked Peter.

"As ready as I'll ever be," I whispered.

Bleep, cheep, and *gurgle.* Suddenly Peter disappeared.

What went wrong? Did Peter get sent by mistake, instead of me?

Then I realized what had happened. Three weeks later in time Peter might be somewhere else. No wonder I couldn't see him.

There was no time to be lost. Rushing out of Peter's garage, I ran over to our house and entered through the back door.

Mother was in the kitchen. When she saw me, she stared. "Angela! I thought you were upstairs taking a shower!"

"Sorry!" I panted. "No time to talk!"

I dashed up to my room. Then I suddenly had a strange idea. What if I met *myself* in my room? Argh! It was a spooky thought.

There was nobody in my room. Where was I? I mean, where was the I of three weeks later?

Wait. Mother had just said she thought I was taking a shower. Down the hall, I could hear the water running in the bathroom. Okay. That meant I wouldn't run into me for a while.

I went to the shelf above my desk and frantically pawed through the junk piled there. I found it! I found the latest issue of the school magazine, the one with the winning stories printed in it.

How much time had passed? Better hurry.

The shower had stopped running. This meant the other me was out of the bathroom. Have to get out of here!

Too late. Just as I started down the stairs, I heard Mother talking again. "Angela! A minute ago you were all dressed! Now you're in your robe again and your hair's all wet! I don't understand."

I shivered. It was scary, listening to Mother talking to myself downstairs. I heard my other self answering something, then the sound of her—my—steps coming up the stairs. In a panic, I dodged into the spare room and closed the door.

I heard the steps—my steps—go past and into my room.

The minute I heard the door of my room close, I rushed out and down the stairs.

Mother was standing at the foot of the stairs. When she saw me, her mouth dropped. "But . . . but . . . just a minute ago you were in your robe and your hair was all wet!"

"See you later, Mother," I panted. And I ran.

Behind me I heard Mother muttering, "I'm going mad!"

I didn't stop and try to explain. I might go mad, too.

It would be great if I could just keep the magazine with me. But, like the spring roll, it would get carried back to its own time after a few minutes. So the next best thing was to read the magazine as fast as I could.

It was hard to run and flip through the magazine at the same time. But I made it back to Peter's garage and plopped down on the stool.

At last I found the story: the story that had won the contest in our grade. I started to read.

Suddenly I heard *bleep, cheep,* and *gurgle,* and Peter loomed up in front of me. I was back in my original time again.

But I still had the magazine! Now I had to read the story before the magazine popped back to the future. It was hard to concentrate with Peter jumping up and down impatiently, so different from his usual calm, collected self.

I read a few paragraphs, and I was beginning to see how the story would shape up. But before I got any further, the magazine disappeared from my hand.

So I didn't finish reading the story. I didn't reach the end, where the name of the winning writer was printed.

That night I stayed up very late to write down what I remembered of the story. It had a neat plot, and I could see why it was the winner.

I hadn't read the entire story, so I had to make up the ending myself. But that was okay, since I knew how it should come out.

———

The winners of the writing contest would be announced at the school assembly on Friday. After we had filed into the assembly hall and sat down, the principal gave a speech. I tried not to fidget while he explained about the contest.

Suddenly I was struck by a dreadful thought. Somebody in my class had written the winning story, the one I had copied. Wouldn't that person be declared the winner, instead of me?

The principal started announcing the winners. I chewed my knuckles in an agony of suspense, as I waited to see who would be announced as the winner in my class. Slowly, the principal began with the lowest grade. Each winner walked in slow motion to the stage, while the principal slowly explained why the story was good.

At last, at last, he came to our grade. "The winner is . . ." He stopped, slowly got out his handkerchief, and slowly blew his nose. Then he cleared his throat. "The winning story is 'Around and Around,' by Angela Tang."

I sat like a stone, unable to move. Peter nudged me. "Go on, Angela! They're waiting for you."

I got up and walked up to the stage in a daze. The principal's voice seemed to be coming from far, far away as he told the audience that I had written a science fiction story about time travel.

The winners each got a notebook bound in imitation leather for writing more stories. Inside the cover of the notebook was a ballpoint pen. But the best prize was having my story in the school magazine with my name printed at the end.

Then why didn't I feel good about winning?

After assembly, the kids in our class crowded around to congratulate me. Peter formally shook my hand. "Good work, Angela," he said, and winked at me.

That didn't make me feel any better. I hadn't won the contest fairly. Instead of writing the story myself, I had copied it from the school magazine.

That meant someone in our class—one of the kids here—had actually written the story. Who was it?

My heart was knocking against my ribs as I

stood there and waited for someone to complain that I had stolen his story.

Nobody did.

As we were riding the school bus home, Peter looked at me. "You don't seem very happy about winning the contest, Angela."

"No, I'm not," I mumbled. "I feel just awful."

"Tell you what," suggested Peter. "Come over to my house and we'll discuss it."

"What is there to discuss?" I asked glumly. "I won the contest because I cheated."

"Come on over, anyway. My mother bought a fresh package of humbow in Chinatown."

I couldn't turn down that invitation. Humbow, a roll stuffed with barbecued pork, is my favorite snack.

Peter's mother came into the kitchen while we were munching, and he told her about the contest.

Mrs. Lu looked pleased. "I'm very glad, Angela. You have a terrific imagination, and you deserve to win."

"I like Angela's stories," said Peter. "They're original."

It was the first compliment he had ever paid me, and I felt my face turning red.

After Mrs. Lu left us, Peter and I each had another humbow. But I was still miserable. "I wish I had never started this. I feel like such a jerk."

Peter looked at me, and I swear he was enjoying himself. "If you stole another student's story, why didn't that person complain?"

"I don't know!" I wailed.

"Think!" said Peter. "You're smart, Angela. Come on, figure it out."

Me, smart? I was so overcome to hear myself called smart by a genius like Peter that I just stared at him.

He had to repeat himself. "Figure it out, Angela!"

I tried to concentrate. Why was Peter looking so amused?

The light finally dawned. "Got it," I said slowly. "*I'm* the one who wrote the story."

"The winning story is your own, Angela, because that's the one that won."

My head began to go around and around. "But where did the original idea for the story come from?"

"What made the plot so good?" asked Peter. His voice sounded unsteady.

"Well, in my story, my character used a time machine to go forward in time . . ."

"Okay, whose idea was it to use a time machine?"

"It was mine," I said slowly. I remembered the moment when the idea had hit me with a *boing*.

"So you s-stole f-from yourself!" sputtered Peter. He started to roar with laughter. I had never seen him break down like that. At this rate, he might wind up being human.

When he could talk again, he asked me to read my story to him.

I began. "'In movies, geniuses have frizzy white hair, right? They wear thick glasses and have names like Dr. Zweistein. . . .'"

ABOUT THIS STORY

Lensey Namioka, who has written stories with Japanese as well as Chinese characters, notes that some Chinese people feel insulted by the Fu Manchu stereotype, but she wanted to have a little fun with that and so created the Lu Manchu role that Peter plays in this story. She also reports she has always been fascinated by science fiction and has wanted to write a science fiction story but never tried one. Now she has.

ABOUT THE AUTHOR

Born in Beijing, China, Lensey Namioka has traveled all over the world and now lives in Seattle, Washington, with her husband, a professor of mathematics who was raised in Himeji, Japan. She is the author of a humorous story about a Chinese teenager titled *Who's Hu?* as well as *Phantom of Tiger Mountain*, a mystery-suspense story set in China before the Mongol invasion. Starting with *White Serpent Castle*, Ms. Namioka has also published a series of novels for young adults that feature the adventures of two young samurai warriors in feudal Japan, including *Island of Ogres* and, most recently, *The Coming of the Bear*. Her newest book, a novel for middle-grade readers, is *Yang the Youngest and His Terrible Ear*, and she is working on a young-adult novel about intergenerational conflicts within a Chinese-American family.

NO GUARANTEES

I SAW
WHAT I SAW

by Judie Angell

Yeah. Well. I'm not dumb. I don't lie, and I'm not one of those nuts, either. Ask anyone, anyone who's known me for the last twelve years, which is all the time I've been alive, if Ray Beane ever, I mean *ever* ran off at the mouth with stupid stuff nobody'd believe. I never did. I always tell it straight. My dad, before he died, that's the way he raised me. And my mom, she's the same way. *Be on the level with folks, Ray, and always look 'em in the eye.*

I live in Poma Valley, California. I was born here, like I said, twelve years ago, and I haven't hardly been anywhere else in all that time. Once, when I was nine—this was just before the Lord took my dad away with cancer—we went on a little trip south to San Francisco. It was just the three of us—my mom, my dad, and me—and we rode on the trolley car and saw some of the sights down there. But I guess that was about the only time I was out of Poma Valley. I have a grandpa from Ohio, but I have never visited him. He comes here sometimes to see us. See? I'm being as straight as I can be about everything, so nobody can say I lied or exaggerated or anything.

Poma Valley is a little town. Very rural, you'd call it. Only about five thousand people. And I go to school in a one-room schoolhouse, just like that old-fashioned program you see sometimes in reruns on TV. It's true. We have the sixth, seventh, and eighth grades all in one room. And there's only ten of us in all those classes. I get there by bus and it takes about forty-five minutes to an hour, depending on the roads and the weather. Cross my heart. I know there are a lot of people who won't believe there are really places like that left in America, but there are, and I live in one. It's real, all right.

I know what's real.

I told you my name, but the whole of it is Raymond Earl Beane, Junior. I was named for my dad, and when I have a son of my own I'm going to name him Raymond Earle Beane the Third. My mom, she laughs and says I'd better have a wife who agrees with that choice, but I don't guess I'd marry somebody who didn't. Anyway, that's my name, and I said my age and mentioned everyone in my family except for some cousins who also live in Ohio, so that's it for my autobiography. We did autobiographies this year in seventh grade. Mine was pretty short.

I stand about five-two and weigh in at about one hundred ten. I'm not very big, but it doesn't bother me. I've got yellowish hair. It's straight and long, sort of, behind the ears. I like soccer and football and I like to listen to country music. Most of my friends like rock, but I like country, and I don't care who knows it.

I have a dog. Maybe I should have mentioned him as part of my family, but I'll mention him now. He's part Lab and his name's Red. He's a black dog, but his name's Red and that's it.

I guess that's enough about me, but I wanted to tell the kind of person I am to help prove out what I say. Hope nobody minds.

The time I'm talking about now, it was six months ago in May. Just getting on to summer. What I wanted real bad was a team jacket. For soccer. I was on the team, and all the other kids had red jackets that said "Poma Valley Soccer" in white on the back with a picture of a soccer ball, and then you got your first name in white script writing put on the front on the left side. Boy, I wanted one, but we just couldn't afford it, Mom and me. See, I had a good jacket, so I didn't really need another one. This was just something I wanted. Around our house we can really just about deal with what we need. "Want" is something else.

So Mom said if I could raise the money over the summer, it'd be okay with her if I bought myself that jacket. And that's when it started.

Our main street, well, it's called Main Street, and like you'd expect, it runs straight through town and then it turns into Route 34 and goes on to skirt by the farms. But there's a movie theater called The Poma on it, along with a pharmacy, a launderette, a Thom McAn shoe store, a hardware store, and a few other shops I can't remember. Oh, right, there's an army-navy store, too, and a diner on the corner. Out a ways in the other direction, there's an A & P and a bowling alley, too, and that's about it for Poma Valley.

The store I didn't mention is the little market between the launderette and the pharmacy. It sells groceries. It's called Meyer's.

I started out looking for work in the bowling alley. I wasn't sure what I could do, but I thought it would be fun to hang out there and maybe get to bowl a few frames every now and then, you know, improve my game. But no luck. So I moved on to the shoe store and the pharmacy (I skipped the launderette—doing the laundry at home is bad enough). I didn't have any luck there either, and I finally ended up at Meyer's grocery store.

We never shopped at Meyer's. Mom says the little markets are always more expensive since they can't buy in bulk the way the supermarkets can, so I had never met Mr. Meyer before. I guess I'd seen him some. I mean, you can't really miss anyone who lives or works in Poma Valley, but I never paid him any mind before that day. Funny thing was, he knew me.

"Ray Beane," he says when I come in. And he grins this big grin at me. I guess my jaw kind of drops and he laughs. His laugh is big and nice, not the kind of laugh where you think maybe he's making fun of you. "Sure I know you," he says. "I like to know who all the kids are."

I found out later that it was true he liked most of the kids, but he also wanted to keep an eye on us. There are plenty of kids who take stuff, rip it off, you know. And if he knew kids, called them by name and treated them nice, maybe they wouldn't do it so much to him. Take stuff, I mean.

He was a smart man, Mr. Meyer, but I didn't find any of this stuff out till later. Till I started working for him and getting to know him.

Yeah, he hired me. Minimum wage plus the tips I'd earn for deliveries. Part-time after school, and when school let out a few weeks later, full-time, ten till six. Sweep the place inside and out, dust the shelves, pack groceries, even wait on customers if he was busy, all the stuff you'd expect would be done in a small grocery store. What he didn't mention was he really wanted somebody to talk to. He talked a lot.

If that sounds as if I didn't like to hear him talk, then I said it wrong. I did like it.

Mr. Meyer's first name was Abe. Abraham. He was Jewish and spoke with an accent. He told me his age—sixty-seven. He was proud of it, he said, because he had been in a concentration camp in the Second World War and any time he lived after that was "borrowed time." He laughed when he said it, but I knew he didn't think it was funny.

Except the thing is, he wasn't at all angry or anything, just grateful. He said he was grateful to have come out of such a dark and terrible time and be able to live in sunny California and run his own business, too.

He didn't have a family. He said they all died in the camp. He showed me two pictures, of a dark-haired woman and a little girl. The pictures were very old—they were black and white, and yellow around the edges, but he was proud of them and kept them in a gold frame in back of the counter.

"My mother," he said. "And my sister." He told me their names, but I couldn't pronounce them. I know that the only time his eyes didn't laugh was when he looked at those two pictures.

The truth was that the store wasn't that busy most of the time. A lot of people must be like my mom and they shop at the A & P. Some folks'd come in for last-minute things like a newspaper or a carton of milk or bread or something, but not too much more. I may have made—tops—three deliveries all summer. But lunchtime was busy. Mr. Meyer made deli sandwiches, and the guys who worked on the roads and the truckers and local folks would come in for tuna salad, bologna, roast beef, whatever, and milk or a soda or beer. I guess that's where most of the money was made, the lunches. Anyway, he never complained about money, Mr. Meyer, so I guess he made enough for his needs. I didn't complain either, because so did I. And then some.

Except for lunchtime, we had time to kill, Mr. Meyer and me. We'd sit down behind the counter and he'd give me what he called his "philosophy of life."

"There's always someone worse off than you, Ray Beane," he'd say. He always called me Ray Beane, my whole name, like it was one word. "It's sad you have no papa, but a mama you have.

There are boys who don't have both, you know. And not only that, your mama, she loves you very much, right?"

"Well, yeah . . ."

"'Well, yeah,' you say. Of course she loves you very much. To have someone to love you is a wonderful thing."

I wanted to ask him who he had to love *him*, except I thought it would be rude. Only he was one step ahead of me there.

"When I was young, I had a whole big family who loved me very much, so I know what it's like. Many people, they never know what it is like to be loved."

I looked at him.

"It's like the optimist and the pessimist, yes? The optimist has a glass of schnapps, he says it is half full. The pessimist has the same glass, he says it is half empty. You see the difference?"

I thought I did, except I didn't know what schnapps was.

"When you wake up in the morning, Ray Beane, what do you see?" he asked.

I thought for a second.

"Uh . . . my alarm clock . . . my closet door . . . Red, lots of times, he wakes me up."

"Do you see the sunlight streaming through your window?"

"Uh, yeah . . ."

"'Uh, yeah.' Does it make you feel good that another day is here? Another day when you can put on your clothes and your shoes and walk around, healthy, in the sunlight?"

"Uh, yeah . . ."

"'Uh, yeah.' Some vocabulary you got there, Ray Beane. We got to do something about that."

"I got an A in Vocabulary," I told him.

He smiled. "Only old men think about being lucky to wake up in the sunshine and walk around," he said. "Kids don't have to think about that. But it would be nice if they did. Just once in a while, Ray Beane. Think about it. It will make you a nicer person."

I didn't see how, but I liked him, so I decided to think about it. Once in a while.

"Did you know, Ray Beane, that ninety-nine percent of the things you worry about never, never happen?" he asked once.

"Huh?"

"It's true. Ninety-nine percent. A fact."

"Sometimes they do," I said.

"One percent. The odds are very good that worrying is a waste of time. And besides, worrying won't change what happens anyway, will it?"

I shook my head.

He shrugged this big shrug. His shoulders

covered his ears. "So why worry?"

That was the kind of stuff he said, all the time. I told Mom about him and the things he said, and she said he sounded like a very wise man. She still didn't shop there, though—she said everything in his place was at least a dime more than at the A & P.

Once my friend Frankie came in for candy. He was with his older brother and they were both acting wise. You know, kidding around, punching each other and ragging on us a little. Frankie was doing it because his brother Jim was there. Usually he's pretty nice. But anyway, I saw Jim lift this Baby Ruth bar off the candy rack. I caught him in the big round magnifying mirror Mr. Meyer has at the front of the store, so you can see what's going on in the aisles. I didn't know what to do. I mean it. If I said something, I'd be dead meat when school started—I knew it. But still, there was Mr. Meyer and how nice he was to me and all—I mean, I always got to take stuff home at the end of the day and he was teaching me things—he made me learn a fact from the encyclopedia every single day and memorize it and tell it to him. He did.

I couldn't stand it. I turned red and my stomach hurt and then before I even knew it, Frankie and Jim were gone, outta there. My stomach hurt worse than before, but I still didn't say anything.

And then I felt a hand on my shoulder.

"It's okay, Ray Beane. I knew they were your friends."

I felt like I was about to cry. Okay, I did cry.

"You're my friend too," I blubbered, feeling like a total wuss.

"A different kind," he said.

"Well, if you saw, how come you didn't say anything?" I asked, wiping my nose on my sleeve and feeling even stupider.

He didn't answer. I knew it was because he was waiting to see what I would do.

"I won't let it go again," I said, real softly.

"I won't put you in that position again," he said, even softer.

Later, after work, I found Frankie. I told him if he ever came in there with Jim again and ripped off Mr. Meyer, I'd personally break his face. I said *his*, not Jim's, because I couldn't take Jim. But I can take Frankie and he knows it, so it was a personal thing, between the two of us, and that way no one at school would have to know and Mr. Meyer wouldn't have to know and Frankie wouldn't let it happen again. I guessed. I hoped. I sort of worried about it every time Frankie came into the store with his brother, which wasn't even that often, but neither of them even flicked a whisker, so Mr. Meyer was right about that—I worried for nothing.

It was what I *didn't* worry about that happened.

It was a Thursday. I know it was a Thursday. I woke up and thought about the sunshine that day. I was grinning all the way to work and I told Mr. Meyer about it and he grinned too. And the day was bright and nice like it usually is, especially in summer. It was morning, before the lunch folks, so the store had its usual few customers. I remember Mrs. Lefton came in and bought cat food and Mrs. Crowley came in for orange juice and bread—she's the housekeeper for old Mr. Staley—and Willy Pelosi bought a paper, two doughnuts, and a black coffee. I remember all of that.

And I remember the truck. It was a red pickup and it pulled up right in front of the store, right there in the sunshine on Main Street, and one man jumped out of it. He was wearing a hat. And then it was fast and blurry and I don't like to talk about it, but this is the way it went.

The man had a gun and he pointed it right at us, Mr. Meyer and me. And he said he wanted money. He knew the old man kept a lot of it in a vault in the back and he wanted it, he wanted it. Mr. Meyer never said a word, but he was holding a can of bug spray—we were stacking them, the ant-and-roach-killer cans; he said they do pretty well in summer—and he suddenly threw it, the can, he *threw* it right at the guy with the gun. He hit the guy and the guy dropped the gun, but not before it went off. And then Mr. Meyer, he picked up another spray can and sprayed the guy's face. The guy was yelling, because of the spray in his face, and I was so scared, I mean, I hope and pray never to be so scared again, but there was Mr. Meyer right next to me, saying, "It's okay, Ray Beane, get the gun, now before he can see again, that's the boy, that's my boy, now hold it on him, I'm right here, we'll hold it on him, we'll do it together, just like we do things."

And he winked at me. He really did. Winked at me. I saw it.

Then I was holding the gun and hollering my head off. Outside I could hear the truck pulling away, grinding gears and blowing soot, and then Mr. Aiken from the pharmacy came in and he was with a whole bunch of people who heard the gun and the yelling and the truck and everything, and the police came and they took the guy away. He was still covering his face and crying or something from the spray in his eyes.

And then Mr. Aiken, he put his arm around my shoulders and took me out of the store. Damned if I wasn't crying again, but I was shaking so bad I could hardly stand, I was still so scared.

"It's okay, Raymond. They've called your mom and she's on her way. It's all right, boy, it's all right," he kept saying.

And the crowd, I could hear the crowd. It was too early for the lunch folks, but they were there anyway—they just appeared, along with the rest of Poma Valley. I remember it all just perfectly, just like it was going on right this minute.

"Nothing like this *ever* happened before in the valley . . ."

"Did too. Last year and the year before."

"That was the gas station got held up. And it was at night, no one was there."

"Was too there."

"Was not and there weren't no gun."

"One of 'em got away."

"Yeah, in a red pickup. They'll get him."

"Poor kid, poor Ray."

"Ray's the lucky one. Poor Meyer, that's who. Poor old guy."

That's when I stopped blubbering.

"What about Mr. Meyer?" I asked.

But instead of answering me, Mr. Aiken just kept patting and squeezing my shoulder. I moved quick, then, and started to head back into the store, but Mr. Aiken and someone else grabbed me and held on to me and wouldn't let me go. So I *really* started hollering then, you bet, just yelling my fool head off for Mr. Meyer to come out. *Come out! Mr. Meyer! Come out! Come out, Mr. Meyer!*

But "Shh, boy" was all Mr. Aiken would say,

and everyone else just seemed to turn away from us, looking down at the sidewalk or up the street into the sun.

"He can't come out, Ray," Mrs. Lefton said. She took Mr. Aiken's place and pulled me away with her arm around my shoulder. "He can't come out, Ray, honey, he was shot. That shot everyone heard, it caught him, honey. You don't want to go back in there—"

But I did, and she couldn't hold me then. Nobody could. I raced past them, pushed past them. There wasn't anybody who could stop me then.

The paramedics from the volunteer ambulance corps were picking him up from where he'd been lying on the floor at the end of the shelf with all the bug sprays. They put him on a gurney, and even though I knew he was dead, I still lost it when I saw them put the sheet over him.

They did catch the guy in the truck. His pal told them just where to find him. He also said how he heard "the old guy" had this safe in back of his store with all this money because Jews always have a lot of money they hoard, and how he knew the store was never busy that time of day, all kinds of stupid and weird stuff like that. I'm trying to say how I remember it all, and I do, anyone can see that, but it didn't come together for me until the police questioned me later. Actually, it was just Captain Ebsen, who sometimes takes my mother out, both of them being widowed. It was when he was asking me all those questions that everyone started looking at me funny.

See, the gun went off just once, and that's when Mr. Meyer had to have been shot. But it was *after* the gun went off that he sprayed the robber's face and told me to hold the gun on him and said we'd do it together, that he was with me. And winked at me.

But everyone said I was too upset to be rational. That's what they said. I wasn't rational, but it was understandable, they said, after what I went through.

Well, yeah, I guess I went through something. And I guess he'll always be with me, that old man and his old pictures and his "philosophy of life." And I don't guess I'll ever really get over what happened to him. I'll remember everything he said about being lucky and about worrying and about the sunshine and about the half-full glass, just like I know he'd want me to.

But after that shot went off, he was *there* next to me, calling me Ray Beane and telling me we'd do it together.

And he winked at me.

I saw what I saw.

ABOUT THIS STORY

Many of the stories in this collection were inspired by real incidents or problems. This story is not based on any real people or events, but the background is authentic. Judie Angell says she once met "the son of an old family friend who lives in a California town exactly like the one in the story. He teaches in a one-room schoolhouse that his children attend." That provided the setting; the story came from there.

ABOUT THE AUTHOR

If you want to find novels written by the author of "I Saw What I Saw," you will have to look under the names of Maggie Twohill, for younger readers, and Fran Arrick, for older readers, as well as Judie Angell, for middle-grade readers. As Fran Arrick, she has published *Tunnel Vision* and a new novel about AIDS called *What You Don't Know Can Kill You.* Her most recent novels written as Maggie Twohill are *Superbowl Upset*—about an extended family's visit to the Super Bowl—and *Valentine Frankenstein*—about a fifth-grade girl who stuffs a Valentine box and makes an unpopular boy a hero. Judie Angell's most popular novels for middle-grade readers are *In Summertime It's Tuffy* and *Dear Lola, or How to Build Your Own Family.*

THE BEST BEDROOM IN BROOKLYN

by Carol Snyder

◆

One day in Brooklyn, where I live, I came home from school and let myself in with the key that hung on a string around my neck—as always. The hair on my arms stood on end. Something was different.

There was a faint smell of perfume, as if someone wearing it had walked by not long ago. My mother hates perfume. So does my married sister and so do I. Except this one didn't smell so bad.

I didn't feel in danger. The door had been locked tight—as always. Nothing seemed out of place until I went to my room. I tossed my books onto my bed—as always. But then I noticed the blanket and pillow were rumpled. I'd left them smooth and neat. My mother insists. I felt like I was in the middle of "Goldilocks and the Three Bears."

"Who's been sleeping in my bed?" I said out loud in a baby-bear voice like when I baby-sit and read to my little niece. No answer. I looked around the room. There was a red-leather suitcase in the corner and a makeup case as well. And a black-lace-trimmed slip hung over my desk chair. My mother is not the black-lace type. There's an extra bed in my room that used to be my sister's before she got married and moved out. Tossed across the bed was a man's brown tweed jacket I'd never seen before.

What was going on here?

Then I heard the front door open and some unfamiliar voices and laughter. I looked around for a place to hide. I grabbed my books and rolled under my bed, hoping I wouldn't sneeze from the dust balls I'd never bothered to vacuum. I'm not in the habit of cleaning under anything. I don't believe in it.

"I didn't know Brooklyn was going to be so beautiful, Charlie, tiny green lawns and red flowers in cement lion pots."

All I could see were high heels as the woman who was speaking sat on the bed I was under and spoke some more.

"It's real swell of your business friends to let us

stay with them spur of the moment like this."

"Mmmm," the man said, not paying much attention to her.

Oh great, I thought. My parents invited businesspeople to move into my room. Nice. And what a fine impression I'll make creeping out all dust covered and scaring them to death. Well, they should have asked me first. It's my room. I waited six years to have a room to myself, one half my life! And now I was just supposed to give it up to Charlie and what's-her-name for who knows how long.

Then, hoping that they might scare easily and leave, I rolled out from under the bed, stood up, and dusted myself off as if people naturally do this every day in Brooklyn.

"Hi," I said. "I'm Lisa. Who are you?"

"My, you gave me a start," the woman said, putting her hand over her heart. She had long red-polished nails without even a chip in them. "Oh, sweetie, we're in your room, aren't we? We'll be real careful with everything. Don't worry. I'm Phyllis and this is my husband, Charlie. You have beautiful blue eyes," she said, touching my chin so she could turn my face to see them better. "Like your father's," she added.

Phyllis had dark eyes lined with pencil like models on magazine covers. Her hair was dark and shiny and had just enough curl in it so if she shook it I bet it would fall right into place.

"Where did you come from and why?" I asked, sitting down on the bed next to her, where she patted at a spot.

"We're from Omaha, Nebraska," Charlie said. "Here on business."

"Nebraska sounds very far away," I said. "You have kids there that you have to get back to real fast, right?"

"No kids," Phyllis said. "It just never worked out for us, having kids. But that's life," she added, adjusting one of her earrings.

"You're my kid. My beautiful kid." Charlie teased Phyllis, grabbing her from the back and giving her a hug. And she turned around and kissed him, laughing.

My parents don't fool around like that even in their own room. I'm sure of it. "So, your hotel room will be ready tomorrow?" I asked.

"Well," Charlie said, "we travel a lot and stay in lots of hotels, but your nice father insisted we stay here and not spend a fortune on hotels. Didn't you see the note your mom left on the kitchen table?"

Nice of my father to invite people to stay in my room, I thought. I didn't notice him giving up his room. "No, I didn't see the note. I haven't been in the kitchen yet," I said.

"Well, let's go, then. Phyllis will fix you something good to eat. Won't you, Phyllis? She's the best cook in the world."

"Let's bake a chocolate cake from scratch," she said, and popped up, taking my hand and pulling me into the kitchen. "We just went to the avenue to that Waldbaum's store and bought the ingredients. Your dad said for us to make ourselves at home, that his house is our house. Isn't that nice?"

I held in my answer.

Well, soon the house smelled delicious and I had chocolate smeared on my face from licking the bowl. And the three of us were laughing and joking as if Charlie and Phyllis had always lived here. It was fun, since usually when I come home the house is empty till my mom and dad close their clothing store at six o'clock and drive out from Manhattan.

Phyllis raved about having such a wonderful real kitchen to work in and cooked chicken à la Charlie for dinner. I helped her roll up the pieces of chicken and put fancy toothpicks in them and make the cream sauce she'd once tasted in a fancy French restaurant in Paris that Charlie loves.

It was fun until I remembered that I would be sleeping on the couch in the living room until further notice and that Phyllis and Charlie would have a room of their own . . . my room . . . the best bedroom in Brooklyn.

My dad made a big fuss over the dinner and the chocolate cake. Mom smiled and kind of eyed the burned pot and the pile of dishes in the sink. She herself much prefers to send out for Chinese food à la Joy Fong and has not made a chocolate cake from scratch since the birth of Betty Crocker.

The next day I could hardly move. I'd watched the late-night movie on TV and the late-late-night movie too. Now I love movies and it was a treat to have the television to myself. But I was really tired and stiff that morning, especially my neck.

But Phyllis knew how to get "cricks out of necks" with a massage technique she'd learned in the Orient or someplace. And before Charlie and my mom and dad went off to work, Phyllis even made light, fluffy omelettes for breakfast. A different kind for each of us. I had tomatoes and cheese in mine. We all raved about them except my mom, who stared at the burned frying pans and sinkful of dishes, which she scrubbed before going off to work. Her nails are not long and painted red.

My mom is more the "bagels or doughnuts for breakfast" type. And a hot breakfast means the bagels get toasted. But she toasts them very well—except for the time she answered the phone and the kitchen filled with dark smoke and set off the detector and my dad used the fire extinguisher and it took us two days to clean up. We haven't had hot breakfasts too much since then.

I went off to school leaving Phyllis to catch up on her beauty rest in MY bed, in MY room.

———

When I came home from school, Phyllis greeted me at the door with a smile. She had baked chocolate-chip cookies and had a glass of cool milk ready for me. We crunched cookies and talked about boys and how they're actually shy sometimes, but that's when they usually do something gross so you won't know it. Then she said she'd bought a home permanent if I wanted her to curl my hair and give it some body. My hair hung limply around my face. "Baby-fine hair," my mother calls it. "Stringy and straight," I call it. The stuff didn't smell great, but I let her do it.

I would never let my mother touch a chemical to my hair. I would be sure it would permanently frizz my hair or change its color. She once tried to cut my bangs, and I needed first aid and a month to get them to grow back straight. Phyllis can do anything. She's perfect.

———

After a few days I was telling my friends all about her. Like how she puts together outfits like in a fashion show. And how she even sews her own hats. She has a framelike gauze hat and she covers it with burgundy velvet and decorates it just so with velvet-covered cherry shapes.

My mother once offered to hem my jeans and she did great, except when I tried to put them on I couldn't because she'd sewed the leg openings together. That's when she found Clara, the dress-maker. I bet if I had a mother like Phyllis, she'd sew all my clothes just right and make me skirts and blouses in the latest styles. And I would be happy on open house night at school, when she would be the prettiest mother there and she would listen to the teacher and not ask a million questions. And I would not be embarrassed because she had on slacks that were too short because she didn't have time to read the label and had put them in the dryer instead of laying them out flat to dry.

"Isn't Phyllis the greatest?" I said to my mom one night.

"Yeah, the greatest," my mom said sarcastically. "I don't know the greatest *what* yet, but she's the greatest."

When my friends would come over, Phyllis would laugh and joke with us like one of the girls, polishing our nails right on the coffee table in the living room even if the remover bottle left a ring on the wood.

It seemed like Phyllis and Charlie would be with us forever. In my closet, my clothes were pushed to one side and Phyllis's and Charlie's beautiful things had lots of space.

And on my dresser, my things were pushed into a corner and Phyllis's makeup and polishes and brushes and lotions and hairsprays and jewelry and scarf holders and nail files and curling iron took up all the space.

And my stuffed animals were piled up in a basket and my scrapbook was stuck up on a shelf. It hardly even seemed like my room anymore except for the wood carving of my name, "Lisa," that still hung on the wall.

And all the kids always wanted to come over after school for fresh-baked carrot cake from scratch or cupcakes baked in ice-cream cones with sprinkles or some neat treat and sewing lessons and jewelry making—all taught by Phyllis. And crab sessions about whose mom did the dumbest things weren't as much fun anymore. I don't even think my friends would have noticed if I was missing.

One day I left them all gabbing with Phyllis and went and sat quietly in my room under my name with the basket of stuffed animals in my lap. I was gone a good hour, just enjoying the privacy. Just enjoying the feel of my own bed under me.

That night, for dinner, Phyllis cooked the best

roast any of us had ever tasted.

The next day, a month to the day of their arrival, Charlie insisted he take us all out to a nice restaurant in Manhattan. So Phyllis and I set out to take the train from the Avenue J station in Brooklyn to Rector Street in Manhattan, like I've done with my mom a million times.

My mom can get anywhere. She never gets lost or frightened of street people. She always gives the homeless lady at the train station some money and wishes her good luck and better times. Then the lady smiles.

Phyllis wouldn't let me stop and give her anything. And she kept asking, "You sure you know what station we get off, Lisa? You sure?" And when the local suddenly switched to being an express and I said, "Uh-oh, we better switch trains," I thought she was going to faint.

And when some ordinary soot got on her white jacket, you'd have thought she was having a heart attack. I was really embarrassed.

When we got to my parents' store, my mom was busy helping customers, adding up bills on the machine, climbing up ladders to get some man a shirt in the right size. And old-time customers would greet her with a hug. She had this wonderful smile and could juggle three things at once and be sweet to everyone.

"Your mother is really something," Phyllis said.

"The way she talks business and uses computers and cash registers and raised a family and looks great without a ton of junk on her face. How does she do it, Lisa?" she asked.

And for the first time I saw Phyllis as she really was. And for the first time I saw my mother as she really was. Each one being the best she could be. Each one her own special self. Each one with different things I could learn from and add to and become my own grown-up me someday.

I ran up to my mom and I hugged her tightly. "I love you, Mommy," I whispered in her ear. "Tomorrow could we order in food from Joy Fong?" I asked.

She smiled at me and whispered, "You got it."

The next day when I got home from school, I rang the doorbell. There was no answer. I let myself in—as always. There was nothing baking in the oven. There were no dishes in the sink. I went to my room. There was no red suitcase or makeup case. My things were all back in their proper place. I opened my closet door. There was plenty of room with just my clothes in it. On my bed was a box with beautiful wrapping and a handmade bow. A card said:

> *To Lisa with thanks for letting us use your room. Enjoy!*
>
> *Love, Phyllis and Charlie*

P.S. Charlie got called away on business suddenly and we're off to Peru. That's life. I'll write. I've learned so much from you and your wonderful family. Please keep in touch.

I opened the package, saving the bow. I hugged the gorgeous white angora sweater and whispered to the air, "Good-bye, Phyllis and Charlie, and thanks."

Mom and Dad brought Chinese food home from Joy Fong and we caught up on news and Mom and Dad thanked me for being so understanding and nice to Charlie and Phyllis. And I thanked them for calling some business friends in Peru and recommending Charlie as a sales representative. And Mom said she'd asked Phyllis for her chocolate-chip cookie recipe and would also bake cookies now and then, but warned that they might not come out as light and wonderful but that we could still bake them together, just the two of us.

"And if worse comes to worst," I said, "we'll use them as hockey pucks." And we all laughed. Together again. Our family—as always.

That night I slept in my own bed. In my own room. And it was wonderful!

ABOUT THIS STORY

"I loved growing up in Brooklyn," Carol Snyder says. There were always interesting people—family members, friends, customers of her parents' business—popping in and out of her house and life. "My room really was taken over unexpectedly, and for what seemed to me then to be endlessly, by a couple much like the characters in this story." The house described here, Snyder reports, also appears in her novel *The Leftover Kid*.

ABOUT THE AUTHOR

Carol Snyder, who now lives in New York City, decided she wanted to be a writer when she was in seventh grade. It wasn't until twenty-four years later that she published her first book, *Ike and Mama and the Once-a-Year Suit*. Since then she has published more than a dozen books for children and young adults, including several other warm and humorous books about Ike and his grandmother and Jewish family life in the Bronx around 1918. In addition to *The Leftover Kid*, her novels about young teenagers include *Memo: To Myself When I Have a Teenage Kid*; *Leave Me Alone, Ma*; and *Dear Mom and Dad, Don't Worry*. Most recently she has been working on several picture books for younger readers and has been taking art classes with the hope of illustrating her own books in the future. She says that *The Goodnight Game* is a good book for middle-grade baby-sitters to read to the two- and three-year-olds they take care of.

A FOOLPROOF PLAN

by Steven Otfinoski

Don't get the idea I'm a regular class cheat. It's true that if the kid sitting next to me during a test happens to be a genius and has his test paper out in full view of half the class, I'm not going to look the other way. I mean, I'm not stupid. But that doesn't mean I spend half my waking moments thinking up new ways to cheat, either.

Before I continue, let me say that my best friend, Joe Luzzi, is a whiz at American history. It's not that he studies any more than I do (which isn't much), but he's got a head for dates and battles and stuff like that. They stick in his brain like glue. I guess it's just something you're born with, like a great pitching arm or a good sense of direction.

Joe has Mr. Dooley for American history the period before I do. Mr. Dooley was planning a big multiple-choice test on the American Revolution on Monday for both classes. This got Joe and me to thinking after school that Friday about how neat it would be if he could somehow give me the answers to the test before I took it. It wasn't something we were actually planning to do. It was just kind of fun to think about it. But that was before Joe came up with his foolproof plan.

"You could slip me the answers between classes in the hall," I suggested.

"But my next class is in the other end of the building," Joe countered. "If I waited around for you, I'd be late for class, and that might get us both into trouble. It's too risky."

I pondered this.

"I could tape the answers under your chair before I left the room," Joe said.

I shook my head. "No good. Someone is sure to see you. Mr. Dooley might even see you. Where would that put us?"

"You're right," sighed Joe. We both thought some more and suddenly Joe's eyes lit up like two Roman candles. I knew this time he had a real brainstorm.

"I've got it!" he said. "It's absolutely ingenious! Foolproof! I'm sorry I didn't think of it myself."

"Didn't you?" I asked, confused.

"No, I saw it in this spy movie on TV," Joe explained. "This spy had to pass on vital information to another spy, but they couldn't risk being seen together by the enemy. So the first spy left the information for the other spy in a public rest room."

"A rest room?"

"That's right."

I was beginning to think that Joe had lost his marbles. "What did he do?" I asked sarcastically. "Write the secret formula on the bathroom mirror?"

"No, of course not," Joe replied. "He put it in the paper-towel dispenser."

"You're kidding," I said.

"Listen, here's the plan," Joe began, lowering his voice as if he might be overheard by foreign agents. "I take the test on Monday morning and copy the answers down on a paper towel. The class ends. I go to the boys' room, open up the towel dispenser, and place the paper towel with the test answers in the dispenser."

"How are you going to do that?" I asked.

"I have a key," explained Joe. "Remember, I'm Mr. Jeeter's helper after school. He trusts me with it."

"Bad move on Mr. Jeeter's part." I smirked. Mr. Jeeter is the school custodian.

Joe ignored my wisecrack and went on. "I lock the towel in the dispenser and leave. You ask to be excused by Mr. Dooley to go to the boys' room before the test begins. You pull out a few paper towels from the dispenser and find the towel with the answers on it. You write them down on the palm of your hand and go back to class. Bingo! Instant A."

I looked skeptical. "It sounds good, but what happens if someone sees you putting the towel in the dispenser?"

"No one's going to see me," Joe insisted. "If someone's in there I'll just wait till they leave. Then I can lock the door. Mr. Jeeter does it all the time while he's cleaning the bathrooms. It'll only take me a minute or two to set the towel in place."

"What if Mr. Dooley doesn't let me out of class?" I asked.

"Have you ever seen Dooley turn anyone down for the bathroom?" Joe asked. I had to admit that our history teacher was a pushover when it came to such matters.

I still wasn't convinced. "What if somebody gets to the towel with the answers on it before I do?" I asked Joe.

"That won't happen," he replied. "I'll put the towel about a dozen in from the bottom. Nobody could go through them that fast before you got there. You just keep pulling them out until you reach the right one."

"What if someone else is in the boys' room?"

"Just wait until they leave," Joe said. "Relax, will you? I tell you, this is foolproof."

It sure sounded like it. I have to confess I was getting as excited as Joe about the whole thing. It wasn't so much the cheating part that captured my imagination as much as the thought of getting away with it so cleverly. Like a couple of professional spies, we went over the plan numerous times that weekend, even timing out the minutes between when Joe went to the boys' room and I left with the answers.

On Monday morning, I walked into Mr. Dooley's history class with a confident stride. I hadn't even bothered to make my usual quick skim of the chapters we were to be tested on. I was planning to rely entirely on our foolproof plan. The risk made the whole adventure seem all the more exciting.

Mr. Dooley made a few announcements and briefly went over our next homework assignment. Then he told us to put away all books and papers. While he was speaking, I shot my hand up and asked if I could use the boys' room. Mr. Dooley looked a little uncertain, and for a moment I thought he was going to turn me down. But then the frown faded from his face and he told me to hurry back because the test was about to start. I promised I would as I took the green-colored hall pass from his hand.

The whole way to the boys' room my heart was beating against my rib cage like a tom-tom. The bathroom was empty, just as Joe predicted it would be. I went straight for the gleaming, metallic dispenser on the tiled wall and tugged on the first brown paper towel. It was blank. I pulled out two more. Not a jot of writing on either of them. Four, five, six . . .

Suddenly I heard the door to the boys' room swing open. I shoved the blank paper towels into the trash barrel and turned on the water. Around the corner of the metal partition appeared pimply-faced Roger Dubroski. Some break! Roger is a real nerd. The trouble is, he doesn't know it. He thinks he's just a regular guy like Joe or me and he tries to act the part. A conversation with Roger gives new meaning to the word *boring*. He was the last person on earth I needed to see right then.

"Hey, Fred. How's it going?" Roger asked. I kept my end of the conversation to a minimum and Roger chatted away as he carefully examined the newest zit on his face. I hardly heard a word he said. All my attention was focused on the paper-towel dispenser.

As Roger talked, I washed my hands in slow motion. Then I pulled out another towel—it was blank—and wiped them off. I was determined to keep wiping them until Roger was on his way out the door. Do you know how hard it is to wipe your hands for that long? Try it sometime. But Roger, bless him, didn't stop talking long enough to take any notice of how silly I looked.

He washed his own hands and then pulled out a towel. I looked at the wet towel in his hands in horror. It was covered in blue ink! Roger Dubroski was wiping his dirty, cruddy hands all over *my* answers to Mr. Dooley's history test! I watched helplessly as he rolled the towel into a small, wet ball and pitched it toward the trash barrel. He missed, of course.

"Nuts!" exclaimed Roger. "Gotta practice that foul shot. How about shooting some hoops after school, Fred?"

"I don't think so," I said lamely, grateful to see that Roger wasn't bothering to pick up the towel. I was afraid he'd notice the writing on it.

"Well, I'd like to stay and chat till lunch," said Roger breezily, "but I gotta get back to biology. We're dissecting frogs today."

"Sounds like fun," I said, faking interest.

"You said it," laughed Roger. "Betty Foreman nearly upchucked when Ms. Chang demonstrated the first incision!"

I would've given anything that moment to be upchucking in Ms. Chang's biology class over a dead frog or any other small animal you can mention instead of returning to Mr. Dooley's history test.

Roger finally left and I snatched up the paper towel from the floor. It was a mess. The blue ink was running all over the place. I spread the paper towel carefully on top of the flat soap dispenser and prayed that no one else would come in to disturb me. (They didn't.) Under careful examination, I was relieved to find that only a few of the answers were totally undecipherable. All the rest were blotchy but still readable.

I neatly wrote each lettered answer on the palm of my left hand with my trusty ballpoint. They just fit. Then I flushed the incriminating evidence down the toilet, like any good spy would, and hustled back to class.

Mr. Dooley gave me a slightly askew look over the top of his tortoiseshell glasses as I walked in. I handed him back the hall pass and he handed me a test.

"You'd better get busy, Mr. Lendleman," Mr. Dooley said. "Your classmates have a head start on you."

I nodded and went back to my desk, smiling

secretly. I skillfully managed to sneak a peek at each answer on my palm and wrote it down in the appropriate space. I took my time, staring off into space occasionally and gnawing thoughtfully on the eraser at the end of my pencil. I wanted to put on a good show for Mr. Dooley, who was watching us with eagle eyes from his desk. When I got to the three questions I hadn't the answers for, I read the questions and found, to my great surprise, that I actually knew the answers to two of them.

When the time was up, Mr. Dooley asked us to put down our pencils and pass our tests in. I followed the instructions and then gave my left palm a few rubs. The sweat from my other hand reduced the answers on my palm to a blue smudge.

As the bell rang, I got up from my chair, full of confidence.

"How did you do?" asked Susan Anders, who sat across from me.

"Oh, all right, I think," I said, grinning ear to ear.

"I don't think I did too well," she sighed. "I hardly studied at all. I have a friend in the previous class and she gave me a few answers in advance. I thought it might help, but it didn't, of course."

I was truly surprised. It appeared that Joe and I

weren't the only twosome who had plotted to make good use of Mr. Dooley's back-to-back testing. I had to play it cool, though. I didn't want to let on about our plan, not even to Susan.

"Why didn't it help?" I asked her warily.

"How could it, when Mr. D. pulled that fast one on us?" replied the girl.

I stopped dead in my tracks, right in the middle of the crowded hallway.

"A fast one?" I repeated.

Susan looked at me, puzzled for a moment. Then she smiled. "Oh, that's right, I forgot," she said. "You were out of the room when Mr. Dooley announced that he had switched the questions around on our test to discourage any cheating between classes."

I could feel my heart sinking to the general vicinity of my toes. "Are you serious?" I said.

"Yeah," replied Susan. "So much for my free answers. Oh well, I'm glad you did well, Fred. Next time I guess I'll try studying."

That makes two of us, I thought.

ABOUT THIS STORY

Steven Otfinoski wrote a version of this story a few years ago for the Weekly Reader Pal Paperback series, but it was never published. This rewritten version is a lighter look at cheating, which the author has examined in another story, "The Answer Man." In that story, a student whispers test answers to his classmates in order to be popular. Otfinoski says it is clear in both stories that "crime does not pay—not even in the classroom."

ABOUT THE AUTHOR

The majority of Steven Otfinoski's books have been nonfiction, including biographies of Lewis and Clark, Mikhail Gorbachev, and Jesse Jackson. His most recent biography is *Nelson Mandela, The Fight Against Apartheid.* But he has also written many humorous horror-adventure stories for young readers, including *The Shrieking Skull* and, his most popular, *The Screaming Grave,* as well as two baseball mysteries in the Southside Sluggers series: *The Stolen Signs* and *Who Stole Home Plate?* Mr. Otfinoski has also written a number of plays and children's musicals that have been performed in New York City as well as in regional theaters and even in Stratford-upon-Avon in England. His most recent play is a one-man show about the American writer Ambrose Bierce.

TAKING RISKS

A BROTHER'S PROMISE

by Pam Conrad

I

Annie watched Geoffrey's every move. Her brother looked very different since he had gone away to art school in Paris. He was almost a stranger, with his new mustache and fancy clothes. She watched him butter his bread while he spoke to their parents, and she imitated the way he smoothed the butter and folded his slice of bread in half.

Her father was speaking in a loud, booming voice. "The *Times* said last week that this Statue of Liberty gift may be a hoax played on the American people by the French. They say it's possible the statue doesn't even exist."

"But, Father," Geoffrey objected, "I've seen it with my own eyes." Annie watched his cheeks flush with excitement. "It towers over the houses on a small Parisian street. It's wonderful! The reason it hasn't arrived here yet has nothing to do with the French people. The problem is with the American people, who haven't collected any money for a pedestal."

"You mean," said Annie, "that when we build the pedestal, they will send over the whole statue?"

"And not until then," Geoffrey answered.

"How long have the statue's hand and torch been here in Madison Square?" she asked. She thought of it rising over the trees just a few blocks away. It had been there nearly all her life, and she was used to it. Until now, until there was talk of sending it back to Paris because there was no pedestal.

"Let's see," her father said, stroking his thick mustache and gazing into the chandelier. "The hand and the torch came over in 1876 for the United States Centennial Exposition in Philadelphia—where, I might add, its presence did little to encourage donations for a pedestal—and in 1877 it was brought here to New York. How old was Annie, dear?" he asked, turning to his wife.

She was pouring Geoffrey more coffee, holding her heavy lace sleeves away from the urn. "Annie was about five, I believe, and now she's twelve, so the statue must have been here for seven years."

"Are you really twelve already, Annie?" Geoffrey asked, suddenly noticing her and smiling across the table. It was that smile that made him so familiar again.

"You missed my birthday as usual, Geoffrey," she teased. "Otherwise you'd know how old I am. Besides, I'm ten years younger than you are, so you should never forget."

"Oh, but I forget how old *I* am," he said, teasing her.

Annie rolled her eyes. "Well, have you forgotten the way to Madison Square?"

"Probably," he replied.

They grinned at each other. Annie was glad he was home, even for just a visit. Now she wanted to go to the Square and up into the torch with him. "Would you like me to lead you there?" she asked.

"Sounds wonderful!" Geoffrey folded his napkin and put it next to his plate. "If you'll excuse us, Mother, Father, we're off to the statue."

"For one last look," Annie added, "before the hand is returned forever to Paris just because the stingy Americans won't make a pedestal for her."

"Don't say that, Annie," Geoffrey objected, pushing his chair quietly under the table. "Nothing is forever."

Geoffrey walked around the table and offered

her his arm. "Well, let's go see her, shall we, mademoiselle? Get your wrap, and we're off."

II

It was a cold blustery morning as Annie and Geoffrey ran down the polished front stoop of their home and started toward Madison Square. Annie kept her cold hands tucked deep inside her furry muff, and she grew sadder and sadder as they walked along.

"What if Father is right, Geoffrey? What if the hand goes back to Paris? We'll never see it again."

"That won't happen," Geoffrey said. "I have a feeling. I just know that someday the Statue of Liberty will be here in New York Harbor, holding a torch in one hand and a tablet in the other. I *know* it's going to happen. You believe it, too, Annie. Your torch will be back, and not just the torch, but the entire lady, as gigantic a statue as you have ever seen, lighting the harbor and welcoming ships and people from all over the world."

They walked quickly in the winter wind, until they could see the torch and the hand in the middle of the Square. It was a sight Annie had seen nearly every day for the last seven years, but when she saw it with Geoffrey it was always better.

"Look at that, Annie. Can you imagine the size

she will be? A nose as tall as you are? Eyes this big?" He motioned with his hands. "What a wonderful day it will be when she's finally in the harbor!"

Annie smiled. "Can you remember the first time we went up inside the torch, Geoffrey? Do you remember?"

"Of course. Mother was furious at me for taking you up." He shook his head. "I can still see her horrified face as her little Annie stood on the railing—held tightly by me, I might add—waving her doll and calling, 'Momma! Momma!'" He tossed back his head and laughed. "You were so funny!"

"Do you know that's the first memory I have in my whole life?" she said. "It's the very first thing I remember—being up in that torch with you holding on to me, and seeing Mother and Father like little people on the ground below us."

"I'm glad," Geoffrey said softly. "That's a wonderful first memory."

Annie felt tears burn her eyes. "Oh, but it's not fair! I don't want it to go back to Paris! I don't want to lose it. We've had so much fun here. What if it never comes back?"

"Nonsense!" said Geoffrey, as they approached the stone base of the statue that loomed three stories above them. They entered the base and started up the narrow staircase that was lit by gas lamps. At the top, they stepped onto a railed, circular walkway. Geoffrey pulled his silver spyglass out of his vest pocket and let her peer through it up and down Fifth Avenue and Broadway. The wind was howling through the metalwork, and the noise of the horse-and-carriage traffic filtered through the park's lining of bare trees.

They shared the spyglass between them, as they had so many times in the past, each quiet in thought. Annie was sure that this was the last time she would stand like this in the great torch overlooking her city. She had an awful feeling that something terrible was going to happen. Something terrible that she couldn't stop. She sighed and leaned on the railing.

"Oh, now, now," Geoffrey said, patting her shoulder. "No sadness today. Try not to think of this as the end, but as the beginning."

"The beginning?" asked Annie.

"The beginning of what this all was originally intended to be, a beautiful statue in the harbor."

"It will never happen," she said.

"Let's make a pact," he said. "I, Geoffrey Gibbon, swear that I will return to this torch someday with you. I promise that one day we'll stand in this very spot, only it will be higher, much higher, nearly a hundred and fifty feet in the sky, overlooking the harbor and all of the city and country of New York, and *that* will be a great day."

"Describe it to me, Geoffrey," she said quietly.

"We'll stand in this very spot," he began, "and when we look over the edge, we'll look down into the statue's huge face. We'll stand right here and see our country spread out before us—the seas, the hills, the people everywhere celebrating and happy."

Annie smiled and looked at him, glad he was home. "You say things so nicely, Geoffrey."

"Now *you* promise," he said.

Annie straightened up and squared her shoulders. "I, Annie Gibbon, promise to come back to this very spot, wherever this spot may be, whenever that may be, with you, Geoffrey. And it will be a great day."

They smiled at each other, and Annie felt all her worries lift from her shoulders, like birds flying away. Then some people came up onto the walkway beside them.

"Do you believe this monstrosity?" one of them said. "Have you ever seen such a ridiculous lighthouse?"

Annie and Geoffrey looked at each other. He winked, and his mustache twitched ever so slightly.

III

It was almost a year since Geoffrey had returned to Paris, and the American papers were brimming with news of a campaign to bring the statue to America at last. Happily, Annie let the wind sweep her across the cobblestone street, weaving her in and out of the slow-moving carriages, and then let it push her up the polished stone steps of her home. Her one hand was jammed into her fur muff, and the other clutched a copy of the day's *New York World.*

The heavy door opened easily, and as she unwound her scarf from around her neck, she began calling, "Mother! Father!" Annie stomped into the parlor, flashing the newspaper at her parents, who sat unusually still on the velvet lounge by the fireplace. "It's really coming! We're really going to get the whole statue, and Geoffrey and I will go up into the torch again, just like he promised, only this time it will be in the harbor, not in the park.

"Imagine!" she cried. "No one thought Americans could raise the money to build the pedestal, but according to the *New York World* pennies and nickels are pouring in from all over."

"Annie," her mother said softly.

Annie rustled the day's newspaper in front of her. "They have a goal of one hundred thousand dollars to raise, and they just might be able to do it."

"Annie," her mother repeated.

"I'm so excited," Annie continued. "I'm going to earn some money and make my contribution. Have you any idea what this means? Geoffrey was right after all.

"Oh, I must write to Geoffrey! He will be so excited! He knew it! He knew it all along!" She looked from her mother to her father for the first time, and then she saw that her mother had been crying and her father was pale.

"Please, Annie," her mother said, her voice shaky and uncertain.

"What is it, Mother?" she asked. "What's wrong?"

"It's Geoffrey, dear," her mother whispered. "Your brother is dead." Annie's mother dropped her head into her hands and began to cry.

"What are you talking about? What do you mean?"

Her father's voice was choked and soft. "He's been killed in an accident, Annie. I can't believe it."

Annie felt frozen to the ground. Her ears were ringing. Her arms grew numb. "What happened?"

"It seems he was visiting with some people in Germany, riding in some kind of motorized vehicle.

It went out of control. He was killed instantly."

"How do you know this?" Annie shouted, not wanting to believe she'd never see her brother again.

Her father pointed to the parlor table in front of him, to a letter beside a box. It had been posted in Germany, and like all Geoffrey's letters it had unusual and colorful stamps, but the handwriting was unfamiliar.

Annie read over the letter—the accident, the death—to the closing. "I extend my deepest sympathy. I'm sending a package to Annie, whom Geoffrey spoke of with deepest affection. It's one of his possessions that I feel he would have wanted her to have. Sincerely, Walter Linderbaum."

Annie reached out and touched the brown box beside the letter. She lifted it and gently unwrapped the paper. It was a wooden box. She pried it open and inside, nestled in cork, was Geoffrey's spyglass. Dear Geoffrey's rare and beautiful spyglass, etched in silver, trimmed in polished wood. She could almost feel the wind howling through the railings of the statue's hand, almost hear the noise of the horse-and-carriage traffic filtering through the trees. She held the spyglass up to her eye and looked out the window through the fine lace curtains. She looked and looked and looked until she could no longer see past her tears.

IV

In a few weeks, Annie wrote this letter to the publisher of the *New York World* newspaper.

Dear Mr. Pulitzer,

I am sending this money for the Statue of Liberty Pedestal Fund. I live near Madison Square, and I used to visit the torch with my older brother, Geoffrey. Geoffrey was an art student in Paris, and he told me all about the statue and how the man who built the Eiffel Tower in Paris also built the foundation of the Statue of Liberty. He told me how the statue towers over the buildings in Paris, and how he used to look at it and imagine it in New York Harbor. We even made a solemn promise to meet in the torch when it was finally here again. He was always completely certain that she would be here one day.

I want to make sure of it. You see, my brother died this year, and although he can't keep his promise to me, I can still keep mine. I've been to see a local pawnbroker, and I sold Geoffrey's rare antique spyglass made of silver and wood that we used for looking around New York City, from up inside the torch. I'm sad to sell it, but I'm sure he'd understand. Please take this money in Geof-frey Gibbon's memory. And please build a pedestal.

Respectfully yours,

Annie Gibbon

Annie's letter was published in the *New York World*, and its heartfelt message touched off a series of contributions in memory of beloved relatives. Annie was proud to see the fund grow bigger every week until, finally, Joseph Pulitzer declared the fund to be complete, and the construction of the pedestal on Bedloe's Island was to begin at last.

V

October 28, 1886, was a cold, drizzly day, but it was declared a holiday, and New York was astir with excitement. Even though the city was in a festive mood, Annie felt uneasy. Her parents had promised to take her to Bedloe's Island to see the statue that had finally arrived and had been assembled on its glorious pedestal, but Annie wasn't sure she wanted to see it. It wouldn't be the same without Geoffrey. If he couldn't see it, maybe she shouldn't see it either, she thought. But she got into the carriage with her mother and father and headed for the pier, where they would take a boat over to the island.

Annie was quiet in the carriage as she watched the holiday crowds out the window. Her mother patted her hand reassuringly. "I guess we all miss Geoffrey this day," her mother said. "He would have enjoyed this."

"Oh, yes," sighed Annie, watching the American and French flags on the fronts of buildings. "This should be Geoffrey's day. He saw the statue in Paris, and he should be here today."

They were all quiet and sad and rode in silence until they reached the pier. Her father found the people who would take them across. Annie boarded a boat with her parents, and they started out toward Bedloe's Island. The harbor was afloat with every kind of boat—from ferryboats and freighters to yachts, scows, and battleships. The steam from all the steamships put a cloud over the harbor, but everywhere there was music— "Yankee Doodle Dandy," the "Marseillaise"—and the laughter of people celebrating.

Annie stood shivering by the railing of the boat. Looming ahead, standing majestically in the center of the harbor, was the shape of a gigantic lady holding a torch in one hand and a tablet in the other.

"You believe it, too, Annie," she could almost

hear Geoffrey saying. "The Statue of Liberty will be here in New York Harbor—the entire lady, lighting the harbor and welcoming ships and people from all over the world." Tears filled Annie's eyes. She was suddenly glad she had come.

"Look," she whispered. "Look at her, Geoffrey."

Annie had never seen so much excitement and merriment in her life. President Grover Cleveland was there, with bands and dignitaries, and there were speeches and songs and cheers and patriotic excitement. She and her parents joined the crowd and listened to the speeches. She was especially excited when Joseph Pulitzer took the stand and gave his speech. He talked about the American people who had finally come through. He talked about the great crews that had built the pedestal, the wonderful French people who had sent the statue to us. He called it the greatest gift one nation ever gave another. The crowd cheered and laughed, and Joseph Pulitzer beamed with pride as if he had brought the statue over single-handedly.

Then, just when it seemed he was through, he looked over the crowd thoughtfully and shouted out, "By the way, is Annie Gibbon here today?"

"What?" her mother gasped.

Annie froze in disbelief.

"Annie Gibbon?" Joseph Pulitzer called once again.

"Here I am!" Annie cried, waving from her place in the crowd.

"Come up here, Annie!" He laughed, and the crowd parted for her. She made her way to the podium, barely knowing what she was doing, barely believing this was really happening. Mr. Pulitzer reached out his hand and guided her up the steps. He kept her at his side and spoke to the crowd.

"I don't know if you folks remember, but Annie wrote a letter to me that we published in the *World* a while ago. Isn't that right, Annie?" he said, turning to her and smiling.

She nodded numbly.

"Well, I'm so glad you're here. You see," he said, turning back to his audience, "she lost her brother last year, a brother who loved the Statue of Liberty. He'd actually seen it in Paris, and Annie sold his special spyglass and sent the money to the Pedestal Fund in his memory. And that led many others to do the same thing."

A few people clapped, and Annie looked down at their faces.

"Annie, I have a surprise for you." He turned around, and someone handed him a long, thin wooden box. "When I read your letter, I sent my people out to all the pawnshops in your area. I said to myself, 'Joseph, when the statue comes over, that little girl is going to have her spyglass back. Yes, she is.' Now you take this spyglass and climb to the top of that lady and take a good look around, Annie."

People were laughing and clapping, and Joseph Pulitzer was nearly bursting with himself. But all Annie could see was the familiar box in her hand. Carefully she opened it, not believing, but, yes, Geoffrey's spyglass was nestled in the box, waiting for her. The band began to play, and Annie looked up into the face of Joseph Pulitzer. "Thank you," she whispered.

VI

Annie's parents walked her to the base of the statue, where they hugged her and let her go up alone. Holding the spyglass box tightly in her hand, she started up the stairway. The inside of the statue was immense, studded with bolts and held together with girders and supports. She remembered how once Geoffrey had carried her up the stairs in the torch. How huge the torch had seemed then, but it was nothing like this! She climbed and climbed and climbed, 161 steps, never stopping at a rest station, and not even stopping at the observation room in the crown.

Then Annie entered the part of the statue that

was so familiar to her. She began to climb up into the raised arm. Her hand touched the cold metal wall; her feet sounded lightly on the stairs. She was alone. Up and up, until at last she stepped out onto the circular walkway around the base of the torch. She felt as if she had arrived home, but only for an instant, and then her breath was whisked away. She had known she would not see Fifth Avenue and Broadway, but there was no way she could have prepared herself for what was before her. She was certain if she reached up she could have touched the gray clouds, yet she clasped the railing tightly with her gloved fingers. The wind whipped around her, whistling through the gratings, and the earth stretched out in all directions.

"Describe it to me, dear Annie," she thought she heard a voice say.

Her words were blown away by the wind, but she began slowly. "When I look over the edge, I can see down into the statue's beautiful face. Her nose is strong and straight, and I can see her lips, proud and determined. The spikes of her crown are huge and studded with bolts. In her hand is a tablet that reads 'July 4, 1776.' I am standing in the torch that symbolizes the light of freedom, and before me I can see my country spread wide and far, the seas, the hills, and the people everywhere celebrating and happy. I can hear the band, and I can see battleships and steamships, and in the distance I see buildings and steeples. On the ground, I can see people like tiny ants."

She smiled, raised her spyglass to her eye, and scanned the crowds below. "I can't even find Mother and Father." Then she turned the spyglass to the horizon. "It's the haziest of days, Geoffrey. It's difficult to see. I'll have to come back again one day." She smiled. "Yes, I'll come back on a clear day, when I can see the hills and the distant horizon. There will be more days, many more, and I'll come back again and again. I promise. You were right, Geoffrey. This is a great day."

Annie stayed as long as she could, until the wind and the cold seemed to be buffeting her from every direction, and then she started down. On her way home, skimming across the harbor in the boat, Annie turned back to the statue and watched her there in the twilight. A few fireworks had gone up in the foggy night, and everywhere boats were lit with bright lights and lanterns.

And then slowly, very slowly, the torch in the great lady's hand began to glow. It was dim at first, and then brighter, until it glowed with a fierce and proud light. Annie watched, and she was certain that from across the dark waters of the harbor the torch light faintly, but surely, winked at her.

ABOUT THIS STORY

Historical fiction, like this story, is always a combination of real events and fictional ones. In "A Brother's Promise," the Statue of Liberty is certainly real, as are the events related to it. The construction of the pedestal, begun in 1883, was interrupted several times because of lack of money. And publisher Joseph Pulitzer did start a newspaper campaign to raise money to complete the work. Annie Gibbon and her brother, as well as Annie's letter and the antique spyglass, however, are fictional. Pam Conrad says her story was inspired by a novel called *Time and Again* by Jack Finney (who also wrote *Invasion of the Body Snatchers*), where the main character is transported into the past and goes up into the hand of the Liberty statue when it is in Madison Square Park.

ABOUT THE AUTHOR

Historical fiction is one of Pam Conrad's favorite types of writing, because she "likes the idea of looking into the past," she says, "to imagine what it would have been like to live then." In *My Daniel*, Conrad takes the reader back to 1885 through the eyes of a twelve-year-old girl whose older brother discovers dinosaur bones in a creek bed on their Nebraska farm. The hard life of prairie farmers, living in soddy homes, struggling to survive, is also described in Pam Conrad's fictional *Prairie Songs* and shown visually in her recent *Prairie Visions*, a nonfiction book about the life and times of Solomon Butcher, a turn-of-the-century Nebraskan photographer. Her most recent publications are a picture book called *The Lost Sailor* and another historical novel, *Pedro's Journal*, the story of a ship's boy on Christopher Columbus's ship the *Santa Maria*.

116

FUTURE'S FILE

by Robert Lipsyte

◆

On Nic Paku's first day at the Universal News Service, he reported to the Station Chief, who looked him up and down, a short look, and barked, "Get me a news peg, kid."

"A news peg?" asked Nic, fumbling at the translation chip in his ear. The Chief spoke an Earth dialect that wasn't taught on The Orphan Ship.

"There's always something wrong with these kids," said the Chief in a booming voice that echoed through the newsroom. "You deaf?"

"No, sir," said Nic, enunciating carefully, looking the Chief straight in the eye as he had been taught. But he felt his body shrinking inside his gray Orphie jumpsuit. He felt younger than thirteen, even smaller for his age. "Sir, I don't know what a news peg looks like."

"Don't know, don't know," mocked the Chief. "If you don't know something that simple, maybe you don't belong here." He turned his back.

———

Five years later and a million miles away, Prince K*L of the Outer Rim twirled his stalks in anger and croaked, "An Orphie dude! This is heavy, man."

"Orphie?" said the Historian General, peering through six of his eyes at the figures on the Past Time Screen.

"From The Orphan Ships," said K*L, his tentacles itching to pound the Past File Transmitter, to send that little dude a message from the future.

"Orphan Ships?" said the General. He hated to admit he didn't know everything, especially in front of the King's thirteen-year-old son, so he tried to make it sound like a test. "Orphan Ships. Data and analysis. Begin."

"Relax, Max, I'll roll the whole ball of wax. Twenty years ago, in 2086, the League of Earth States began picking up all the homeless kids on the planet, all the kids whose families had been wiped out in wars and plagues and famines, loading them into spaceships and sending them out to the space colonies."

"How barbaric!"

"Some people thought it was for their own good, a chance to start a new life. Most of them would have died of starvation, or spent their lives in the Children's Camps. Some Orphies became slaves on the garbage planets. But the lucky ones were put in homes on remote planets and became trainees in jobs they might like to study for"—K*L pointed down at the screen—"like my little homey honeybunch Nic."

"Homey?" The General tapped at his wrist interpreter. "You are mixing up expressions from various North American time periods and social groups. Homey is an expression used by African-American male Earthlings in the years between 1985 and 1995, while honeybunch is a . . ."

"Fab, Freddie," said K*L, bored. He blinked the Past Time Screen into Scanning Mode and watched the past five years rewind, slowing only for hurricanes and earthquakes on garbage planets. It was his all-time fave, watching trash smash.

———

Nic felt hot and cold as he searched the newsroom for a news peg, dodging the robot cameras and the rolling anchor chairs and the floating files. The reporters and producers and editors and clerks all looked away from him, as if they didn't want to get involved. Afraid of the Chief. *Okay,* thought Nic, *I'll just find it on my own. But what does a news peg look like? Could it be an actual peg, like a hook hanging from a wall?*

"Find it yet, kid?" shouted the Chief. His voice

sounded like the afterwhine of an old garbage rocket, the kind that passed The Orphan Ship at night and woke them up. Nic shuddered. If this job didn't work out, he'd be going back to The Ship, and it could be a long time before he got another chance to find a home.

"See what the know-it-alls on Earth do?" the Chief boomed. "They stick you with a human when an android does a better job, and then it's a kid human and, worst of all, one of THOSE kids."

———

"This pig is radically gross," said K*L. "Let's bust his chops."

"NO!" thundered the Historian General. "You know the rules. We never ever meddle, ever. The Cosmic Historical Association monitors the past, it does not manipulate it."

K*L touched the Past File Transmitter. "So why this, Big Guy?"

The General's wings fluttered, he was cranking for a speech. "Type Ten Emergency Only—Survival of a Species. Only then are we allowed to send a message to the past, and then only a message that has already been sent, one that is future to them but already past to us. In other words . . ."

"Bo-rrringg," said K*L, pretending to look away as his tentacles ached.

———

The newsroom is like The Ship, thought Nic, *like*

The Camps, like the back alleys before I got picked up. You can never relax, always bullies on your case, you've always got to be ready to fight. He felt a tap on his shoulder and whirled around, fists up.

"Hey." She had a nice smile in a brown face. She raised her hands as if to block his punches. "Don't feel bad. He gives everybody a hard time."

"Doesn't bother me."

"Sure." She offered both pinkies in friendship. "I'm Alison."

"I'm Nic." But he touched her with his thumbs only. Never get too close. "So, what's a news peg?"

"Oh, that's an old journalistic expression. Sort of the peg on which we hang the tale. For example, next year is the Hundredth Anniversary of the Great Garbage Storm, the famous one when a place called New Jersey, in what used to be called the United States of America, simply lifted up and disappeared. So if the Universal News Service decided to run a series on great garbage disasters, hmmm, not a bad idea"—she tapped into her palm computer—"that anniversary would be our news peg, our reason for doing the story."

"Got it," said Nic. "Thanks." He took a deep breath and turned away.

Alison whispered, "Good luck."

Nic marched right up to the Chief's desk. He waited a long time before the Chief turned around and snarled, "You got three seconds and six smart, snappy words."

Nic gulped and said, "News peg equals the new in news."

"That's seven words," sneered the Chief. "Go work with your new friend over there." He jabbed his thumb toward Alison. "If you mess up, you're history and she's in trouble."

"I'll do my best, sir."

"It won't be good enough. You Orphies think the universe owes you a living."

———

"Gag me with a spoon!"

"Why do you insist upon using these late twentieth-century American adolescent expressions?"

"'Cause I'm with the band," said K*L. Got to send that poor boy a message of hope. That creep is-was making his life miserable. Adults! Never want to be one! He wished he was home in his tank with his comparative-words cubes.

The General cleared his communication tube. "You understand, K*L, that a creature your age has never before been allowed in the Society's screening rooms."

"Well, excuuuuuuse me."

———

Alison took Nic up to the cafeteria for lunch.

"The Chief's a dictator," she whispered. "He doesn't want to be here any more than the rest of us."

Nic tapped his translation chip to make sure it was on. "Why wouldn't anyone want to be here?"

"You kidding?" She made a funny face. "This nowhere asteroid is just one step above a toxic-waste dump. Everybody wants to get to Earth, where the real action is. Do you know what we do here?"

"News Relay Station," said Nic. It seemed so important, so powerful.

"Fancy title for directing traffic. All the news stories from all over the universe, print dis-patches, picture stories, thought messages, they're all beamed here and we sort them out and send them to the proper desks on Earth. We're just file clerks, not real journalists."

"Sounds pretty good to me," said Nic.

She smiled and touched Nic's nose with her pinkie. No one had ever done that before. "You're a good kid. I'm going to let you handle the Garbage files. It's the big story these days—there's real trouble cooking. You'll learn a lot."

Nic felt so good, he almost gave her a pinkie back.

———

"I've got to give the Nic-ster a hand," said K*L.

"You don't have hands," said the General.

"It's an expression," said K*L. "Got to reach out to that mellow fellow."

"Don't even think about it," said the General

sternly. "History must be history. The Transmitter is to be used only in the most . . . ah . . . ah, . . ." The General's heads vibrated: He was getting a message he couldn't refuse. *Must be Dad checking up on me*, thought K*L. *Got to work fast.*

"No sweat, daddy-o," said K*L, as he scrolled the Past Time Screen back to 2101, then fine-tuned to Nic in the newsroom scrolling through his own screen for garbage stories. *Ol' Nic works so hard*, thought K*L, *what can I do to make my main man look good for his boss?*

Yo! Stop the presses! Flash! Gonna sit right down and send him a story nobody else will have for another two years.

———

Nic's eyes were watering from scanning the screen, searching for the word GARBAGE, when it finally appeared. His fingers stabbed at the keyboard. He was in too much of a hurry to read the file carefully.

MEDIA ALERT/ January 14, 2103

A fleet of warships from the League of NonCommitted Planets is approaching SANGERTOWN, DRIK4, to stop garbage ships from the Omicron Galaxy from illegally dumping.

As Alison had taught him, Nic centered the

document on the computer screen, punched DUPE, and tapped one copy into the GARBAGE file and another into the Chief's reading monitor. When Nic turned, Alison was nodding and smiling. He had followed instructions perfectly. For the first time all day, he felt his shoulders relaxing. This might work out. He just might find a home here.

"STAFF!" boomed the Chief.

Alison signaled Nic to follow her as editors and producers and reporters and clerks hurried to the conference room. The Chief strutted to the front of the room, waving a copy of the document.

"Now we'll see if you people are worth your bottled air," he growled. "We finally have a story here. What do you want, Oswami?"

"Something's wrong," said Alison. "I've been following this story, and it should be at least another two years before those ships are . . ."

"What do you know?" sneered the Chief. "This could be WAR! In our territory. Put this miserable station on the news map. Get me the Chief of the Planet Desk."

———

"That was your father on the wave," said the General, coming out of his trance. "He said you were a fine youngster who needed discipline and direction." The General touched his left antenna to K*L's center stalk, a friendly gesture but one he would never have dared make without the King's permission. "You must put aside your childish ways, study politics and science and the history of great leaders, not roll 'n' rock—"

"Rock 'n' roll," said K*L before he could stop himself.

"Whatever. Someday, K*L, when the stars of the Outer Rim are in your hands . . ." The General's heads spun as his eyes jumped at the Past Time Screen. "WHAT HAVE YOU DONE?"

———

"JANUARY 14, 2103!" The Chief's eyes bulged. "That's two years from now. Who's trying to put one over on me?" When everyone looked away, he yelled, "The Orphie Kid!"

"Don't blame him," said Alison.

"It's your fault, too," the Chief growled. "You'll never be anything more than an archives clerk. And you're fired, kid. Out the door before I throw you out the window."

———

What a mess! How'm I gonna save my good buddy?

"First, your royal promise," said the General, "that you will never again violate History."

K*L made sure two tentacles were crossed behind his back. "My royal promise." The third tentacle inched its way to the Transmitter. *One* *last message for Nic so he'll know he's got a future. Hang tough, partner. Gotta split.*

Later.

———

Nic left the newsroom before anyone could see the tears in his eyes. Don't give them the satisfaction, he thought. Orphies are tough. Orphies can make it without help from anyone. But he wished he had touched pinkies with Alison.

He didn't see the file taking shape on his screen.

June 21, 2123 —GORBYVILLE, EARTH—Nic Paku named Editor-in-Charge, Universal News Service. Former Orphan Shipper Paku was the only Galactic Correspondent to have ever interviewed the mysterious Emperor of the Outer Rim, K*L. Editor Paku's first official action was to promote longtime asteroid file clerk Alison Oswami to Chief of the Planet Desk.

–30–

ABOUT THIS STORY

Robert Lipsyte was once a copyboy like Nic "for twenty-three wonderful/horrible months" at *The New York Times.* He was, he says, oppressed by malevolent copy editors. "Did I have a future? Could I stand this abuse?" This story, says Lipsyte, "has been rattling around in my head for thirty-five years." Mr. Lipsyte is now a major sports columnist for that same newspaper.

ABOUT THE AUTHOR

In addition to writing for *The New York Times,* Robert Lipsyte became a reporter/interviewer for the CBS television program *Sunday Morning with Charles Kuralt* and was later an Emmy Award–winning host of *The Eleventh Hour* on New York City's public television station. He also wrote *The Contender,* which since its publication in 1967 has become one of the modern classics of young adult literature. Alfred Brooks, the young black boxer of that book, appears again in one of Lipsyte's most recent novels, *The Brave.* As a drug-busting police officer, Alfred Brooks is in the position to help a self-destructive young boxer named Sonny Bear learn to control himself. Among his other well-liked novels for young adults is *One Fat Summer,* the first of three books about Bobby Marks, who is patterned after the author. Robert Lipsyte's most recent novel is *The Chief,* a sequel to *The Brave* that includes the characters from the *One Fat Summer* trilogy.

WILLIE AND THE CHRISTMAS SPRUCE

by Larry Bograd

That year, the frost and snow came early. We dug our way out of four heavy storms before Thanksgiving. People with time and money were talking of skiing. "The best conditions in years." Not for us, though.

We lived on a northern Vermont farm, the four of us Johnstons, plus my older sister Kate's baby daughter. Which meant we got by with selling fresh milk, potatoes, homemade cheese, and maple syrup.

The best time to harvest sap to be turned into maple syrup is the spring. Usually in late March or early April, when the days are warm enough for the sap to flow up from maple tree roots to the trunks.

And there's a second, shorter sugaring season in the fall. The sap in the fall is not as sweet as in the spring. Still, to pay for our Christmas and to get us through the winter, we had looked forward to a good fall run: our farm shipping out enough syrup to soak thousands and thousands of pancakes and waffles, and we Johnstons seeing just enough profit to make it till the spring thaw.

But that year the early and hard cold stopped the flow of sap. The short fall sugaring season was the worst in memory.

"Stupid frost," Kate said, driving with Dad and me and the few cases of fall syrup we had originally kept for ourselves. It was the week before Christmas, and Dad's buyer had called in a panic.

"Nothing we can do to change the weather," Dad said.

"Oh, like acid rain is just a myth," Kate responded. "Like the hole in the ozone won't get any larger."

Kate's sarcasm had become edgier since she had returned home a single mom. I was too tired to remind her that not everything was Dad's fault. If anyone did, I was the one who had reason to complain. Not only was I sharing my room with Kate again, but we were now sharing it with her ten-month-old baby, Shelly, who cried at night.

We were delivering our syrup, all six cartons,

to the wholesaler in White River Junction. The wholesaler reported a bad fall sugaring season all around. The fancy retailers in tourist towns were screaming for additional shipments. He paid Dad in cash and wished us a merry Christmas. The times we had money, we'd stay for some Chinese food in a shopping-mall restaurant off Interstate 91. That day, however, we had orders from Mom to stock up on staples and return straight home.

"Did you even make expenses this year?" Kate asked Dad as we loaded sacks of feed, bags of dry groceries, cartons of baby formula, needed hardware, and loaves of hard salami into the old pickup truck. We'd just spent what money the wholesaler had given us. "Come on, Dad, tell the truth."

"What with replacing a broken vacuum pump and replacing the roof on the syrup house, with hiring an extra man, given all the repairs—no."

No sooner had we left White River Junction than the truck started to act up. Kate had the accelerator down, but the pickup, choking every few minutes, could barely maintain a speed of forty miles per hour on Interstate 91.

"Better get off the highway," Dad told her, "and take U.S. 5 in case we need help."

Although this would add an hour to our drive north, I didn't mind. I liked the old two-lane road that followed the course of the Connecticut River. Watching the dashboard gauges, Kate drove us through a dozen New England towns with their steepled white churches, village greens, and country stores. Past East Thetford and Fairlee, Bradford and Wells River, toward St. Johnsbury. The road was clear but icy and dangerous. The limbs of bare birch trees were coated with crusty week-old snow. The river, a frozen gray, like trapped smoke, looked so cold that I wondered how fish could survive.

"The cost of being alive is simply so high." Dad sighed, his hands slumped in his lap. We'd been silent for most of the ride. I'd thought that he'd been napping. "Truck going to make it?" he asked Kate.

"It could use some new spark plugs," she said.

"Truck could use a major tune-up," Dad said, offering a grin.

"We could use a whole new truck," I tried, and the two of them laughed.

Dad, feeling better, put his arm around me. Pretty soon we'd turn off on our road. Not the state's road. Not the county's. *Our* road. Then up the hill, assuming Kate—and the truck—managed a wicked hairpin turn. Then straight for the lights of our two-century-old stone farmhouse.

I had lived nowhere but that farm in Vermont. In fact, in all my eleven years I'd been to Boston a very few times, but never anyplace bigger. We lacked the means to go elsewhere.

Our farm had been our family's for four generations. I suppose my folks had enjoyed a few good years when I was young. I remember new clothes and a shiny red tricycle. But at least since I'd started first grade, times had been hard and recently had become much worse.

Dad glanced at me. "Willie, maybe next Christmas for those new snowshoes."

"Hey, Willie, trust me," Kate said, tapping my leg for attention. "Given this family's luck with money, you'll be lucky to see those snowshoes for Christmas Year 2093."

My nineteen-year-old sister Kate hated being home again, even with Mom getting stuck in the house with baby Shelly while Kate looked for a job. For all her effort, there were no jobs. Not in our town. Not anywhere close.

Being eight years younger, I grew up almost a doll to Kate. She helped bathe me and no doubt changed plenty of diapers. She taught me "Patty cake, patty cake, baker's man . . ." She helped me learn to ice-skate backward on our frozen farm pond. She read to me the one summer she loved books better than boys.

But by the time she turned fifteen, it seemed like I rarely saw her. Always scampering off to meet friends. Always close to our mom but having loads of harsh words with Dad. Particularly about boys. Time and again, she warned me about letting our folks stick me with the farm.

The road leveled. We approached our bright-windowed house. With luck, we'd unload the supplies and sit down to warm food before it got really dark.

Dad looked across the road at the group of spruce trees growing at the crest of a snowy rise. "Willie, tomorrow you and me need to pick out a tree to bring inside."

It was a family tradition that one of our spruces served as the Christmas tree, decorated with ornaments collected by my mother and by Grammie before her. Ornaments in honor of children's births. Tiny wooden figurines dangling from hooked wire. Fragile colored glass the thinness of paper. In town we never saw trees as lovely as our spruce.

"Is it okay for me to have an idea?" I asked when Kate turned off the truck engine.

"There's a first time for everything," she joked.

"What's on your mind, son?" Dad asked.

"Well, maybe there's some money in the spruces," I said, ready to be hailed a genius.

134

"Don't you know, money doesn't grow on trees," Kate said, ever the smart mouth.

"Son, go ahead," Dad said, eyeing Kate to mind herself.

"Well, Christmas trees in town fetch thirty dollars apiece," I said. "Bet in Boston they'd sell even higher."

Dad sat there and considered. Kate stared at me like suddenly her younger brother had actually displayed some intelligence.

"Your mother would never allow it," Dad finally said. "I'm needed around here, and don't even think about going yourself, Kate. No way we're sending a young woman out alone with an old truck."

But, amazingly, Mom thought it a wonderful solution. Providing that Kate had some escort. Someone to watch over her and make sure the money got home. I could hear Mom and Dad talking it out late that night. Long after the last log had been added to the cast-iron stove. I could hear them because I lay awake, woken by Shelly's mucus-thick coughs.

It was a rule not to disturb them unless convinced of a prowler or bleeding to death. Not that my parents seemed to do much but wear socks to bed and watch TV. Still, figuring that the lack of family finances was an emergency, I threw back my covers.

"Mom, Dad, can I come in?" I asked meekly outside their door.

"Is the baby okay?" Mom asked.

"Kate's been up with her a few times," I reported.

"Son, you can't sleep," Dad said. He was pretty good at stating the obvious.

"Mom, Dad," I said, entering, "how about if I go along with Kate to sell the trees in Boston?"

Mom gestured me over. Her skin smelled of lotion. Her flannel nightgown looked silly but warm. She wanted a hug before sending me back to bed. Before saying, "Very well. Now understand that your dad and I letting you two go to Boston is a one-time thing. Hear? So be extra careful and keep your purpose in front of you."

In the morning, after tending the cows and hens, splitting another three cords of firewood, my arms and back stiff and sore, I helped Dad cut down the spruces. Another frigid, cloudy day. Except for our bright-orange vests, the colors were gray and dull white.

We left the pickup on the snow-packed road, not daring to get it stuck. We walked from there, leaving quick, deep bootprints in the hillside snow. Dad carried the two-man saw. Not casually over his shoulder, but low, in one hand, serious.

"Shame about these trees," he said.

136

"Come spring, we can plant something new," I offered.

We worked the saw. Back and forth. Smooth. Working as a team. For the first time ever, I did most of the effort. Either I was growing stronger or Dad was getting much older.

The first tree cracked and dropped, shaking its blue-green short needles free from snow.

"Figure that's an eighty-dollar tree in Beantown," Dad said.

Bent low, sawing just above the snowline, we felled another tree.

"Tell them these are grown in Vermont, U.S.A.—not trucked in from Canada," he said.

"Okay, Dad."

Another tree fell. The wind, kicking up, soon took care of loose needles and sawdust. Another spruce cracked and dropped, and another. The truck bed was filling and we didn't stop for lunch.

It was dark by the time we cleared the last spruce. The bootsteps we had left hours earlier had grown brittle as we traced them back to the truck and drove home. With Dad's help, I took one spruce off the truck, which we would decorate that night after supper.

Mother insisted I take a bath before bed. She didn't want any Bostonian thinking her boy was a slob. The bath itself was glorious. Hot and soothing. Enough steam to fight off the airy chill. It was the first time in a week that I'd fully taken off my long johns.

Sent to bed, I couldn't sleep until Kate and our parents had a long last tug-of-war over the mud-pit that was my sister's life. When she came in crying, I pretended I was already asleep. She lifted Shelly from the crib and moved to the rocking chair. There Kate sang a lullaby that put both the baby and me to sleep.

Wasting no time the next morning, Kate woke me early. "Come on, Willie. Mom and Dad want us home before supper."

Way before sunrise. "Can't I sleep just a little more?"

She handed me my corduroy pants and a clean flannel shirt.

As I dressed and tried to wake up, Kate lifted a sleepy, snotty Shelly from the crib. In the dim, chilly room, Kate carried her daughter to the rocking chair. Then she pulled the blanket there around the two of them. Feeding the baby a warmed bottle, Kate softly sang:

"Hush-a-bye,
Don't you cry.
Go to sleep, my little baby.
And when you wake

You shall take
All the pretty little ponies. . . ."

"Isn't she special?" Kate asked me. "God, I hate seeing her sick." She had Shelly against her chest, burping her.

"She's special," I said, buttoning my cuffs. "Okay, I'm ready." Kate gently put Shelly back in her crib.

We didn't bother waking our parents. The cold as we walked to the truck snapped me alert.

We drove with headlights for the first two hours. Almost no traffic heading south on U.S. 5 except for all-night rigs and a few locals either getting home or leaving to an early work shift. Crossing the Connecticut River at Wells River and into New Hampshire, we drove through the snowy White Mountains just as the sun gave them shape, getting on I-93 south near Lincoln. The radio began to pick up a rock station from Concord. Kate cranked the volume loud and I didn't mind.

The truck seemed all right, even on the interstate. The sky was clear of clouds. We stopped for a quick lunch in Derry, almost to the Massachusetts state line.

Back behind the wheel with an hour or so yet to go, Kate looked exhausted. "Sorry I'm not old enough to drive," I told her.

"I don't mind the driving," she said with a shrug.

"Then what?" I asked, hoping Kate would tell me.

She sighed. "I can handle that I made a mess of my life. But I hate doing the same to Shelly. She's not even a year old. Can't even afford to buy her a Christmas gift."

"She's so young, she won't remember," I offered.

"Hurts all the same," Kate said, "because *I'll* remember."

We were quiet for miles. The number and hurry of cars, vans, and trucks passing us almost put me in a trance.

"So, how many trees we end up with?" Kate asked. She was changing the subject. Which was okay with me.

"Twenty-five decent ones," I said.

"All six-footers?"

I nodded. "Dad figured eighty bucks a tree. So that's"—I was pretty good at math—"two thousand dollars!"

"Not bad for a day's outing," Kate said, impressed. "I figure we give eighteen hundred back to Mom and Dad and keep the rest. One hundred dollars apiece."

This was a lot of money. Like a full year's allowance.

"What if we get even more for the trees?" I said. "Like a hundred, two hundred each!"

"Maybe this Christmas will be good, after all," Kate said, smiling at me.

"You know my best memory of Christmas?" I said. "How we'd go eat too much food in town. Run around with all the cousins. Eat too many sweets and talk to grown-ups. Then fall asleep on the long drive home. You and me in the backseat, like mummies in our snowsuits. Getting carried inside the house by Mom or Dad. And waking up warm in our own bed."

Kate nodded. "I remember."

Before we knew it we saw our first sign for Boston. I had a road map opened on my lap, but the choices were coming too quickly. "What did that sign say?" I asked.

"Route One and Tobin Bridge!" Kate shouted. She was losing patience with her navigator. "Willie, do we want it or not?"

"No . . . yes. I don't know. Better get off."

Kate did so, only to be confronted with another quick decision. "Storrow Drive. Cambridge. Downtown. Willie?"

"Try Storrow Drive, Cambridge," I said, making a guess.

Kate had to do some aggressive driving, ignoring the honks and threats of other drivers, to try and get over to the left-hand lane to exit. Just then, a delivery van sped and cut her off, nearly causing a wreck.

"Jerk!" Having no choice, Kate took the next exit, and we found ourselves near Haymarket and Faneuil Hall, a mess of twisting streets crammed with cars and pedestrians and mounds of cleared snow.

"At least there's a lot of people," I said. At first I thought a hockey game or movie had let out. Then I realized just how many people—and different ones—were crammed together. I saw more people in that first hour in Boston than I had in my entire previous life. All bundled against the cold wind blowing off the harbor.

"And nowhere to park," Kate snapped back. She turned left, then left again, and we found ourselves in the North End, a hopeless maze of narrow, one-way streets. Cars double-parked to let passengers off in front of Italian restaurants and shops. "Look, isn't that Paul Revere's church?" I asked.

"We're here on business," Kate reminded me.

Somehow we found ourselves crossing the Charles River and heading into Cambridge. "Finally," Kate said. "Let's get to Harvard Square."

After getting directions at a service station, we

found Massachusetts Avenue and followed it into Harvard Square, where a mass transit station, stores, and the famous university met.

Finding a parking place on Bedford Street, Kate went to phone our parents, while I unloaded the trees. I leaned them against trash cans, against short metal fences, against No Parking signs and apartment building walls.

"Hey! Are these your trees?"

Our first customer!

"Make me an offer," I told a young man in wire-rimmed glasses and a ski parka.

"I'm not interested in buying a tree," the guy said snootily. "I'm interested in why you're deforesting our planet."

"First off," I heard Kate say, approaching us from the back, "these trees are from our farm. We cut down a total of twenty-five. Which is probably a lot less than you waste in a given year. And secondly, we need the money. So if you don't like it, just move on!"

"Oh. Okay, I'm sorry," the young man said. "Listen, you won't have much luck here. Most of the students are already home on break. Go into Boston and try Back Bay or along Beacon Street."

So I reloaded the trees and we headed off. We were a mile or so from Harvard when the truck sputtered and seized.

"What the—?" Kate began to say. But before she could finish, the truck died. "Stay here," she instructed me. "I'm going to find a garage."

Sitting there, Kate already gone a half hour or longer, I felt like crying. But what would that help? So I decided I might as well get out and drum up some business. Boy, I thought, will Kate be impressed if she returns to find that I'd sold a tree or two. And sure enough, as if a prayer answered, a slick-haired man wearing a long overcoat slowed to admire the trees.

"Hey, sir, aren't these great-looking trees?" I said, moving in place to stay warm. "Cut just yesterday on our Vermont farm. Every one a beauty!"

"You talk to Tony?" he asked, keeping his hands in his coat pockets.

"Tony?" I asked.

"Where you from?" the man asked.

"Vermont," I answered. "Is there a problem?"

"Are you supposed to be here? On this block?" he asked, confronting me.

"Mister, I don't want any trouble," I said, holding up my hands.

"Well, we control this part of the territory," he said. "And we don't appreciate outsiders thinking they can sneak in and sell trees. Now I'll give you the benefit of the doubt. Which means you have fifteen minutes to get out of here."

Luckily, Kate and a tow truck arrived in ten minutes.

"Boy, what a place to live," I muttered as the operator lifted our truck up behind his.

"Maybe the farm isn't such a bad place," Kate said. "And get this—I sweet-talked this guy and he'll fix our truck, if it's nothing too serious, in exchange for a tree of his choice."

A new set of spark plugs, an adjustment of the timing belt, and new air and oil filters, and we were back on the road, if one tree less. Unfortunately, it was nearly dark. No way would we get home as planned. Following Memorial Drive and crossing the Charles River, we found ourselves in a ritzy part of Boston. People were heading into expensive shops and fancy cafes.

Miraculously, Kate found a place to park, and I jumped out and took down only one tree. A nice, full spruce. One tree, in case we had to move on in a hurry.

Staying in the cab, Kate motioned me to stop the first rich-looking person. Which I did.

"Want to buy this gorgeous tree?" I asked a woman in an ankle-length fur coat. The strange-looking dog she was walking wore a legless sweater.

"Where did you get it?" the lady asked. She

stopped as her dog sniffed a mountain of bloated trash bags.

"From my family's farm," I said. "In Vermont."

"What's wrong with it?" she asked, eyeing the perfect spruce.

"Nothing. It's a beautiful, healthy tree," I said. "Freshly cut just yesterday. Here. Feel how soft the needles are."

"Well, how do I know it doesn't have worms? Or that it wasn't sprayed with some cancer-causing pesticide?"

"We wouldn't do that," I assured her. "We got dairy cattle. Which means we don't spray our land with anything harmful. And it's a healthy tree. I guarantee it."

"To tell you the truth, with all I have to do, we haven't gotten our tree yet," the lady said, sounding interested. "Do you deliver?"

"Yes, ma'am. That's my sister in the truck."

"It is a lovely tree. Promise me that it wasn't stolen."

"I promise. My dad says it's worth eighty dollars," I said, trying to land a sale.

"Do you take credit cards?" she asked. I shook my head no. "A check with a guarantee bank card?" she then asked.

"Sure," I said, not sure. "A check will be fine. Make it out to—"

146

Just then, a police officer interrupted, "Got a license, son?"

"A license?" I repeated, unsure. "My sister has a driver's license."

The lady returned her checkbook to her purse. "I'm sorry," she said. "But I need to get my dog home." With that, she hurried off.

"Lady! Lady!" I called, following her down the street, only to be ignored. Returning to the truck, I kicked the bumper, not caring that I hurt my foot. "Now look what you did!" I shouted before realizing I was talking with a cop.

Kate, though, saw what was happening and was out of the cab in a snap, stepping between the officer and me. "What seems to be the problem?" she asked.

"Miss, I need to see your commercial license," the officer said, keeping his calm. Inspecting the trees, he asked, "Where are the tags? The interstate permits? You can't simply set up a business in Boston without first obtaining the proper papers."

"Officer, please," Kate said. "We didn't know. Please let us sell our trees."

"Please, mister," I chimed in.

The cop stared at me, then at Kate, then at our truck still loaded with trees. "Well . . ." he said with a grin, "it's nearly Christmas. Tell you what.

Just make sure that you two are gone by the time I return in an hour."

"Thanks. Thanks a lot."

For the next fifty-five minutes Kate and I worked like crazy. Ringing doorbells. Taking a scented sprig and letting people have a whiff of the wonderful piney aroma. There was no time for food, no time to rest. It was frustrating trying to get strangers to listen, but worse yet would be to return home empty-handed. When someone offered us fifty dollars, when another offered forty, we took what we could get. We had no time to haggle. Fifteen dollars? We took it, none too happy. How about ten? I'm afraid so. Tree after tree was lifted off the truck, until the last one was sold for five dollars. Some people lashed their new tree to the roof of their cars, others dragged them down the street, leaving a sweeping path in the snow.

Our faces and fingers and toes frozen, we took some of the money and bought ourselves some clam chowder to go. "So how'd we do?" Kate asked as she drove the truck toward I-93 north.

I counted the money, then counted it again. "Four hundred and sixty-five dollars," I told her.

"Not bad for a couple of amateurs," she said with a grin. "You keep ten and I'll keep ten, and we'll give the rest to Mom and Dad."

So our trip to Boston wasn't a total flop. What sadness I felt at losing the spruces was made up by knowing we'd have enough money to get us through the holidays.

By the time we had driven clear of the city, it was nearing ten o'clock. The traffic was quiet. For the most part, people were in bed, long asleep.

"Are you all right to drive?" I asked Kate.

"I'm fine," she said and I believed her. "Quite a one-day adventure," she added. "And to think we thought we'd come home with two thousand dollars!"

This wasn't that funny—but we both laughed.

"Well, the money will help," I said.

"Call me crazy, Willie," she said, "but I think the worst to happen has already happened to me."

"Buy something for Shelly," I said, handing her a twenty-dollar bill.

"Are you sure?" Kate asked.

"Yes, I'm sure. Something warm for the winter. So maybe she—and you and me—can sleep at night." I bunched up a blanket and used it as a pillow against the side door.

"Willie, I'm glad we had this day," she said. Again I waited for some smart comment to follow. But there wasn't any. Instead, we rehashed the day, remembering things to tell Mom and Dad.

I don't know exactly what time we arrived home. I don't remember because I soon fell asleep in the truck and slept most of the way.

I don't recall my sister Kate carrying me inside. But she said she did and that's good enough for me.

I do remember waking up in my own warm bed. Waking up to the smell of our own maple syrup and to pancakes cooking.

That next morning, with the trip to Boston and back already a dreamlike whirl, I looked out my window, expecting for just a moment to see the spruces across the road. Instead I saw the stumps like small grave markers in the snow.

This sad image might have stayed with me if I hadn't walked into the living room and seen our own Christmas tree, tall and decorated. For then I realized that people in Boston were waking to admire the beautiful spruces they had bought from Kate and me. Trees that their neighbors and friends would envy. Trees that children would dress with strings of paper chains or popcorn, with tinsel and their own special ornaments.

Trees that would bring to the dense heart of winter the reminder of life, full and fragrant.

ABOUT THIS STORY

While driving through New England several years ago, Larry Bograd picked up a young hitchhiker who talked about his ill-fated trip to sell Christmas trees in New York City. "Willie and the Christmas Spruce" was inspired by that hitchhiker's story.

ABOUT THE AUTHOR

Larry Bograd is a professor of English at Metropolitan State College in Denver, Colorado, the city where he was born. His interest in the West is evident in two of his novels, *Los Alamos Light* and *Travelers*. He is also the author of nine other books for children and young adults, including *The Kolokol Papers* and *The Better Angel*, which is based partly on his own romantic experiences as a senior in high school. His experiences working at a shelter for runaways in New York City provided the background for *Bad Apple*. His first book for children was *Felix in the Attic*. Most recently for younger readers he has written *The Fourth-Grade Dinosaur Club*, about schoolyard racism; *Bernie Entertaining*, about a boy who wishes to become an astronaut; and *Poor Gertie*, about a girl living with her mother during hard times.

TAKING A CHANCE

by Jan Greenberg

I met Jonathan for the first time on one of those rotten, no-good days when nothing seems to go right. For starters, there was the baseball fiasco. It was our team's first big game. We'd been practicing for weeks. I can still hear Coach Patterson's voice as I ran past him.

"Go get 'em, Teddy. Two outs. Bases loaded. We need a hit."

"Yeah, sure," mumbled Cass Fisher. "Fat chance with Cautious Cooper." The other guys snickered. I tried to ignore them, but by the time I reached home plate, my palms were sweating. Top of the ninth. It was up to me. I knew if I could manage to hit the ball, I could get to first base. There was nothing wrong with my running, but so far my batting average had been a big zero.

The pitcher sneered in my direction and started winding up. I held my breath. The first ball looped high and wide. It was so slow, I decided to give it a whack. But I hesitated a second too long. It popped over my head and flew behind the plate.

"Foul ball," the umpire called. "Strike one." I could hear muffled groans from the sidelines, along with some scattered applause. The next pitch was perfect. But I didn't swing. My arms just wouldn't coordinate.

"Strike two."

Suddenly there was no sound on the field. It was as if someone had turned down the volume. I moved into position, stretched my arms back, and waited. My body felt tight, as if I was tied in a straitjacket. "Come on. Come on," someone yelled. The ball whizzed toward me, and in that moment between action and inaction, I froze. Like the statue of Babe Ruth in front of the stadium, I remained motionless in midswing.

"Strike three. You're out." It was all over.

"You're hopeless, Teddy," yelled Cass as I trudged off the field. The other team started cheering and jumping around.

Coach Patterson pulled me aside. "Listen, Teddy. You can't keep hanging back. You could play ball if you'd just take a chance."

"Sure, Coach," I said. "I'll try." I'd heard that speech before. *Be more aggressive. What are you afraid of?* My father must have said it a hundred times.

I walked home alone, wondering why I was such a big loser, wishing I could quit the team. But the truth was that I loved baseball. Sliding into third base, catching a fly ball, and throwing it home—the pros made it look so easy. Unfortunately, I didn't seem to have the hang of it. At the same time, I have a stubborn streak. I must have inherited it from my grandma Sophie, because by the time I reached my house, I was determined to practice until I dropped. With the bat in one hand, I threw the ball up in the air with the other and swung as hard as I could. It bounced at my feet and then rolled into the rose-bushes a few yards away. Jasper, my bulldog, scrambled after it.

"Give me the ball," I commanded. Instead, he gripped it in his jaws and pranced at my feet, daring me to tug it away. Bulldogs were bred in England to chase cattle and drag them back to the herd. Jasper's grip was so strong, it was practically impossible to pull anything out of his mouth.

"See the bone. Over there," I shouted, trying to

divert his attention. Jasper cocked his head and dropped the ball. As I grabbed for it, he pounced. The ball rolled into the street with Jasper barreling after it.

"Jasper, no! Get back here," I shouted. A car rounded the curve, heading straight for him. Suddenly out of nowhere a figure appeared and, in that split second before the car sped by, tackled Jasper and rolled with him out of danger.

As the boy pulled himself up, he lifted the ball, twirling it expertly on one finger, and tossed it back to me. "Thanks. That was amazing!" I said, breathing a sigh of relief.

"What kind of dog is he?" asked the boy, scratching Jasper's ears.

"A bulldog," I answered. "Most people think he's ugly."

"Then I must not be most people," he said, grinning shyly. Short and stocky, with dark, curly hair, he wore a pair of tattered jeans and a beat-up leather jacket. I'd never seen him in the neighborhood before. "Do you know where Glory Cooper lives?"

"Sure," I said. "Right here." I pointed behind me. "I'm her brother, Teddy."

"I'm Jonathan Briggs," he said, staring past me at the house. "It sure is big." I gave him a second look. Glory's boyfriends were usually tall and preppy. I could hardly tell them apart. Jonathan Briggs didn't fit the mold. I liked him right away—maybe because he had saved Jasper, but there was something else. As he stood there, hands in his pockets, rocking back on his heels, I could tell he wasn't sure whether to stay or go. He was hesitant, edgy like a stray cat. I'm shy myself, so I can recognize the signs. Before he could change his mind, I shoved him toward the door.

"Come on in. Glory's up in her room."

I have to admit, as girls go, my sister is pretty. She flew down the stairs, her long blond hair swinging around her face.

"Hey. It's you!" she said to Jonathan with a big smile. I was shocked. Glory usually acts so cool around her boyfriends. She ushered him into the study and closed the door. Glory knows I'm a snoop, so on went the stereo full blast.

That night at dinner I described Jonathan's brilliant rescue in detail. "Jonathan who?" asked my mother. "Is he that rumpled-looking boy I saw leaving when I got home? He didn't even stop to introduce himself." My mother is very big on manners.

"Jonathan Briggs. You don't know him. I met him in biology class."

"Briggs?" said my father absently. "Isn't there a

Briggs' Laundry in town? Strange nervous fellow who owns it."

"That's Jonathan's uncle," said Glory. "He lives with him over the store. I don't think Jonathan likes him much."

"Where are his parents?" Mom said in a disapproving tone.

"I think they both died a long time ago," said Glory. "I really feel sorry for him."

"It's nice of you to take an interest in someone less fortunate," said my mother. "But I wouldn't get too involved with him. He probably has a lot of problems. By the way, I talked to Margie May today. She says her Danny is quite taken with you."

"He's a nerd," said Glory. For the rest of the dinner, she picked at her food and pouted. This time I was on her side.

Within a week Jonathan became a fixture around our house. He usually showed up right after school and managed to stay through dinner. He worked nights at the laundry. My parents were polite, but they spoke to him in the tone they used for salesmen at the door or people calling the wrong number. I must say Jonathan didn't make it easy. He'd eat everything in sight, but hardly ever said more than three words. Those three words usually had something to do with food. Soon Glory was treating him like all the rest of her boyfriends—bossing him around, taking him for granted. Jonathan, on the other hand, was smitten, hanging on her every word. If she wasn't home, he'd wait for hours.

Those were the times I liked best. We started playing ball in the backyard. Jonathan was the best player on the high school team. He could hit the ball farther than anyone in town. Thanks to him, I started improving. When we weren't playing catch or hitting, we'd roughhouse with Jasper.

"My uncle won't let me have a pet," he told me one afternoon. "Thinks animals are dirty."

"They are," I said. "Look how Jasper drools and sheds all over the place."

"I'd clean up the mess," said Jonathan wistfully. "You and Glory are really lucky." He paused and let out a long sigh. "One of these days, if I can raise the cash, I'm going to split."

"Why, Jonathan?" I asked. "What's wrong?"

"Nothin' you can do anything about, sport," he said, cuffing me on the head.

"Where would you go?"

His eyes took on a distant look. "I'd like to hike up in the mountains, find a cabin in the woods. Maybe in Colorado."

"I'd come visit," I said. "We could go fishing."

Jonathan laughed. "Come on, let's hit a few.

Remember, keep your eye on the ball and don't lurch forward."

I missed it three times in a row. The fourth time I just stood there and let the ball whiz by.

"Teddy, why did you do that?"

"I don't know," I said. "It's better than striking out all the time."

Jonathan threw his glove down and charged over to me. "You'll never get it right unless you go for it. Take a risk. Do you want to play ball or not?" The next time I hit the ball so hard, it flew over the fence. I jumped up and down, I was so excited.

"Way to go," Jonathan shouted. "Try it again. And remember, focus all your attention on the ball." It was starting to get dark when he finally said, "I have to work at the laundry tonight. Doesn't look like your sister's going to show in time."

Glory arrived home a few minutes later.

"Where were you? Jonathan couldn't wait any longer."

She shrugged. "I have other friends besides him." I could see the handwriting on the wall.

Sunday morning. Mom set the glass table in the sun porch. She slapped down the placemats as if they were cards in a game of hearts. Grams was coming for brunch. "Bring in the dishes for me, will you, Teddy? And go wake your sister." She glanced at her watch. "It's almost eleven thirty. Someone has to pick up Grams."

"Last time you made me drag Glory out of bed, she threw a lamp at me." Stacking the dishes into one big pile, I staggered back to the porch and let them slide onto the table. Mom held her breath. Waking my sister was more of a challenge.

"Leave me alone," she shrieked, tossing her pillow. I ducked just in time.

Later, Grams hobbled in wearing a wide-brimmed straw hat with a bright-red ribbon and white gloves.

"You look snappy," I told her, as she handed me a box of See's candies. "Wow! Thanks, Grams." She was followed by a scowling Glory.

"I had my uncle drive me all the way to the airport to buy this for you. Your grandpa loved chocolate too." Her uncle is younger than she is by a week. She calls him Uncle Irv, and they drive all over town in her old black Buick. Grams leaned hard against me as I led her onto the porch to sit down. There's an odor about her of mothballs and gardenia perfume. We sat side by side without saying much. She kept nodding as if someone were talking to her. A fly buzzed over our heads. Outside, Jasper chased a squirrel under the bushes. Just as Mom set a big platter of eggs and bacon on the table, Jonathan ambled in, his hair all tousled as if he had just rolled out of bed.

"Hi, Mr. and Mrs. Cooper," he said, nodding at Glory.

"Just in time for brunch," Mom said, rolling her eyes. "I guess you'd like to join us?"

"Sure. If it's not too much trouble." He looked over at Glory for approval. She shrugged. I pushed another chair to the table.

"You haven't met my mother," said Dad, pouring Jonathan some orange juice.

"Pleased to meet you," mumbled Jonathan.

"Mrs. Cooper's a bit deaf," added Mom. "You need to speak louder."

She passed him the platter. He heaped his plate with food and wolfed down five pieces of bacon as if it were his last meal. I wondered if Mom would say anything, but she just clicked her tongue. Jonathan didn't seem to notice. Grams did and offered him another muffin.

"The boy's got a good appetite," she said. "Just like your father. No matter how much I cooked, the icebox was always empty."

"Refrigerator, Grams," said Glory, but she didn't hear her. Dad launched into a discussion of the stock market, directing most of his comments to Jonathan, who kept repeating, "Yes, sir."

"Tell us your IBM story again, Grams," I said

loudly. Grams looked puzzled, as if she couldn't remember. Her false teeth clacked as she bit into a muffin.

"When Grams was just a young married," explained Dad, "she bought a few shares of IBM through her ladies' stock club. Then she stuffed the certificates in a drawer and forgot all about them. For forty years!"

"That's right," said Grams, perking up. "Now that IB whatever-it-was is worth a fortune."

"No kidding?" said Jonathan. He stopped eating for a moment, he was so impressed.

"You ought to go out and spend it, Grams," I said. "Have yourself some fun."

Grams sat up very straight. "I wouldn't touch a penny. I'm saving it for my grandchildren."

"Right on, Grams," said Glory, giving her the thumbs-up sign. Then Jonathan started asking Dad all kinds of questions about the stock market. I'd never seen him so animated. When Mom and I cleared the table, Jonathan insisted on helping. Then he asked Dad if he could have a word with him in private.

"He's going to ask to marry you," I said, "now that he knows you're an heiress." Glory gave me a snarly look. As we rinsed the dishes, I remembered Grams was sitting at the table all by herself.

"Someone help her up," said Mom. Jonathan beat me to it.

"I'll drive Mrs. Cooper home for you," he said, walking in with Grams hanging on his arm. "I borrowed my uncle's truck today."

"Just call me Sophie," said Grams, handing him her purse to carry. It weighs a ton because she carts all her jewelry around in it. I watched them walk carefully down the back steps. Jonathan leaned his shaggy head closer to Grams, who squinted into the bright sunlight. They were both smiling as he helped her into the truck.

Dad stopped by the kitchen on his way to play golf. "Jonathan asked me to do the strangest thing. Said he'd saved about two hundred dollars. Could I invest it in IBM for him, he needed to make a lot of money right away."

"What did you tell him?" asked Mom.

"I told him I would, but I couldn't promise quick results. After all, it took Grams forty years."

The next day after school, Glory burst in the door, slamming her knapsack on the counter. I was doing equations in my math book. A very satisfying activity now that I finally understood them.

"Didn't you think it odd that Jonathan didn't come back yesterday after he took Grams home?" she demanded.

"Not really," I answered, although I'd waited all afternoon hoping he'd be back to play catch with me.

"You'll never guess. I really can't believe it." Glory snapped the tab off a can of Diet Pepsi. I was munching on See's candies, retrieved from Mom's hiding place in the top cabinet.

"Honestly, Teddy, do you have to take bites out and put the pieces you don't like back? There's a whole gross row like this." She tossed a half-eaten piece into the sink.

"Why don't they make more caramel squares?" I said. "They always fool you with butter brickle. Anyway, where was old Jonathan? He didn't even show up for dinner."

"He stayed at Grams'. All afternoon. Just talking. Then she fixed him her famous 'cooked to death' dinner."

"Dried chicken, lumpy mashed potatoes, and mushy broccoli. Ugh!" we both said in unison, giggling. I had a mental picture of Jonathan slouched in one of those heavy mahogany chairs in her musty dining room. He must have felt completely out of place.

"I'll bet she talked his ear off about all her aches and pains," continued Glory, shaking her head.

I wondered if Jonathan talked to Grams about

his aches and pains. Sometimes I noticed bruises on his arms and scratches on his face. His uncle was big and scary-looking. "What else did he say?" Now I was really curious.

"He said he was taking Sophie out for dinner next time."

"Sophie? I wonder what Mom and Dad will say when they hear about it."

"Hear about what?" Mom banged through the door carrying her briefcase in one hand, a bag of groceries in the other. I tried to stash the chocolate box under the table, but it was too late. "Teddy, you'll spoil your dinner eating all that candy."

"Grams has a boyfriend," I said, partly to distract her but more to see her reaction.

"Don't tell me. Let me guess. Robert Redford? No. Arnold Schwarzenegger. Move away, Jasper, before I trip over you. Honestly, this kitchen is a mess."

"Jonathan Briggs," I said.

Glory looked pained. "He's exaggerating, as usual. Grams made Jonathan dinner last night. That's all."

"How very peculiar," said Mom. Then she went into the study and closed the door. I knew she was calling Dad at the office.

The following Friday our team had a big game

with the guys from Riverdale. It was our first match since I'd lost the last one. I'd had a stomach-ache all day. Jonathan had promised to come, but Glory hadn't been very nice to him lately. I wondered if he'd show up. When I got to the field, he was surrounded by all the guys. I could tell they were impressed when we walked off together. "How are you doing?" Jonathan asked. "Nervous?"

"Nope," I lied, clenching my fists.

"You'll be great. Just remember not to lunge over the plate or clutch the bat so hard." He gave me a big pat on the back. "I brought this for you. It's my lucky charm. My dad gave it to me before he died."

He pressed something cold and hard into my hands. A silver dollar. "Gosh, thanks," I said, stuffing it into the pocket of my uniform. I could feel my hands relax a little.

Somehow that afternoon I could do no wrong. It helped to hear Jonathan cheering me on from the stands. He gave me the thumbs-up sign whenever I glanced his way. Each time I went up to bat, I'd look at the pitcher and mentally call him every name in the book. Then I'd do the same for the ball. For once, I didn't stand there like a stone. Unless a pitch was completely out of whack, I swung at every ball. It worked. I made three base hits. No home runs, but at least I didn't strike out. Even Cass Fisher told me "Good game," after we won three to two.

Not long after the game, Jonathan and Glory broke up. She told me to say she was out if he dropped by. Jonathan took the hint right away and wouldn't even stick around to play catch with me. I felt bad. He was the only one of Glory's friends who had ever acknowledged my existence. But my sister discarded boyfriends as easily as junk mail, so that was that.

I didn't see him again until one day in early May. By then all the trees were in bloom. The colors had changed from muddy browns to green practically overnight.

I was walking home from school, turning the corner near Walgreen's, when a familiar black Buick rolled by. I spotted Grams in one of her big floppy hats. I looked for Uncle Irv. Instead Jonathan sat at the wheel. Grams was chattering away; he was smiling. I wondered what they were talking about. Seeing them together put me in a bad mood. Why was Grams with Jonathan? I felt left out, as if he'd dumped me and Glory instead of the other way around.

A few days later Jonathan turned up on our doorstep. This time he wasn't smiling. In fact, he looked terrible. His left eye was black and blue, his face puffy. "What happened to you?" I was still mad, as if he'd deserted me in favor of Grams.

"Had a fight with my uncle," said Jonathan. "Is your dad around?"

"It's four o'clock on a Thursday," I said. "He's still at the office. Glory's here though." He bent over to scratch Jasper, who licked his hand. "Should I call her?"

"Yeah, sure," he said without much enthusiasm. But when Glory appeared, I could tell by the way his voice turned all soft and mushy that he still liked her.

"Wanna take a walk?" he said.

"Are you all right, Jonathan?" asked Glory. We both stepped outside. He sank down on the grass.

"I want your dad to sell my IBM stock," said Jonathan. "But I can't reach him."

"Why?" she asked. "You just bought it."

"I'm leaving town," he announced. "I can't stay here anymore." We didn't have to ask why not.

"It's not enough money for you to live on," said Glory. "At least not for very long."

He thrust his hands in his pockets and shrugged. "I know, but I'll find another job."

"Teddy, go play with Jasper," ordered Glory. "This is a private conversation." I expected Jonathan to defend me. Instead he nodded in agreement.

"Why don't you move in with your new best friend, Grams?" I blurted out. As soon as I opened my big mouth, I was sorry. Jonathan lay back on the grass and put his arm over his face.

Glory said in a shrill voice, "What does he mean by that?"

"Sophie needs someone to take her places. Her uncle can't always do it, that's all. Besides, I like to keep her company. She's lonely by herself all day."

"She's *our* Grams," said Glory in a hard voice. "*We* can keep her company." We'd only seen Grams once in the last month, when she'd come over for a quick Sunday brunch.

Glory loomed over him. She hadn't bothered to sit down. "Sophie needs things done around the house, and I can use the extra money," said Jonathan.

"Taking money from an old lady!" Glory spat. "I don't believe this." She swung on her heels and stalked back inside. I really felt like a jerk, but I didn't know what to say. So I sidled off with Jasper trotting behind me and left Jonathan there, lying on the grass. When I looked back, he was gone.

Jonathan must have patched things up with his uncle. As far as I knew, he didn't leave town. But he didn't move in with Grams either. There were no more unexpected visits to our house.

Spring turned into summer, and before I knew it sixth grade was over. Since my batting had improved, as well as my nerve, the guys were calling me every day to play. We met at the pool in the morning and played ball all afternoon. For the first time I felt as if I belonged. I should have called Jonathan to tell him how great I was doing, but I never did. I figured if he really wanted to know, he'd call me. Glory had a summer job at Dillard's department store and spent all her earnings on weird clothes. She went on dates every night, but there wasn't anyone special.

One night at dinner Dad said, "I stopped by Grams' after work and guess who was there, washing her windows?" I took a big gulp of milk. Glory pursed her lips. We both knew what was coming next.

"That friend of Glory's, Jonathan Briggs. In fact, I sold his IBM stock and thought that was the last I'd see of him. But it seems he's over at Mother's all the time. She says he helps her out."

"You mean Jonathan? I hope he's not taking advantage," said Mom. "Your mother doesn't always know what's going on. And she stashes money and jewelry all over that house."

"Grams gives him money," Glory said. As soon as the words were out of her mouth, I knew there'd be trouble. I started to speak up, to defend

Jonathan, but the words stuck in my throat. My mother pushed her chair back and stomped away from the table. Later I heard her and Dad talking in hushed tones to Grams over the phone.

I was right. There was trouble, but it didn't happen the way I expected. A few days later on a hot Friday afternoon, I stood on the lawn, hosing Jasper off with cold water. Glory and Mom had just come home from work. Suddenly Dad's car swerved into the driveway; the brakes crunched and he slid out, slamming the door behind him. He rushed inside, his tie flapping against his chest. I ran after him. "What's going on?" For an instant I thought Grams had died. Or the stock market had crashed.

"Ruth," he shouted. "I need to talk to you." Mom appeared at the top of the stairs, followed by Glory.

"Ed, why are you home so early? What's wrong?"

I hung back at the front door, trying to calm Jasper, who started barking. Dogs can sense trouble.

"Ridgely, the trust officer at the bank, called me. Said my mother just marched in there and signed over some stock certificates to a young man they didn't know. Insisted on it. They were concerned because the kid looked disheveled, as if he'd been in a brawl."

"It had to be Jonathan," gasped Glory. "I don't believe this!"

"What could Grams have been thinking? We'd better see if she's all right," said Mom.

"I'm calling the police to pick him up," said Dad, "and then I'm pressing charges."

All three began jabbering at once. A loud furious chorus. I knew they wouldn't listen to me, but I had to do something. I couldn't hold back this time. I edged out of the house and broke into a run. As I picked up speed, I crisscrossed through the Wrens' yard, pounding over bumps in the grass, and slid under the fence. The Wrens' German shepherd pulled on his chain and growled. I could hear my breath coming in short gasps.

"Please be there. Please be there," I repeated to myself. My chest tightened from fear, from running so hard. When I finally reached the center of town, I made a beeline for the laundry. I spotted Mr. Briggs behind the counter. His big hulking frame and grim expression made me stop short. I made myself push through the screen door.

"Is Jonathan here?" My voice sounded like a hoarse squawk. But I knew Mr. Briggs heard me, although he barely glanced in my direction.

"Boy's gone. Took off this morning and I haven't seen him since." Then he thumped his fist on the counter. "He better be back by eight or else!"

Down the sidewalk I raced, weaving in and out among shoppers, dodging cars to cross Main Street. A few minutes later I reached Grams' house. The door was unlocked, so I pushed in without even knocking. Grams was rocking back and forth in her favorite chair, reading the newspaper.

"My, Teddy," she said, looking up. "What a nice surprise!"

"Grams," I cried, "where's Jonathan? He's in big trouble."

"Come over here," she said. "I can't hear you."

"Grams. It's Jonathan. Dad's having a fit about those stock certificates. He's calling the police. This is serious!"

"You mean my IBM? Don't worry, Teddy. I have enough money for you and Glory. But Jonathan needs some of it. That crazy uncle of his!"

"I don't care about the money," I shouted. "But Dad thinks Jonathan stole it."

Grams stopped rocking and slowly pulled herself up. "Sit down, Teddy, and calm yourself. First I'm going to make us some tea. And then I'm going to tell you a story." I knew we didn't have time, but when Grams decides to repeat one of her stories, there's no stopping her. I collapsed on

173

the couch and let out a ragged moan. Grams returned with two steaming mugs of tea and settled back in her chair. In a slurring voice with traces of an accent, she began.

"When your grandpa and I left Germany right before the war, we had to flee quickly before the Nazis arrested us. We'd seen the trains go by, heard the stories of Jews being transported to camps. It was 1937, before your father was born. We grabbed what we could—money, jewelry, clothes—and drove across the border into France. Then we booked passage on a big ship for America. On the boat we slept on cots, crowded in steerage with immigrants from all over Europe, mostly Jews, escaping Hitler.

"One morning we awakened and before us, shining over the sea, was the Statue of Liberty. Everyone clapped and cheered. We could see the skyline of New York City with all its tall buildings in the distance. But when we looked around for our suitcase, it was gone. We had been robbed during the night."

"That's awful, Grams," I said. "Did you report it?"

Grams shook her head. "There was nothing we could do. We were starting a new life with no money, just the shirts on our backs, as Grandpa liked to say. But a relative, a cousin we'd never even seen, met us. He and his wife let us move in with them, shared what little they had with your grandpa and me. Later we moved to Illinois and opened our first store."

What's this have to do with Jonathan? I wondered. *Why is she telling me this now?*

Grams' bony hand reached for mine. "Listen to me and listen good, Teddy. All these weeks Jonathan's been doing little chores for me, fixing a broken pipe, running to the market. At first he wouldn't take a penny. I insisted. Then I noticed those black-and-blue marks and I knew a terrible thing was happening to him. He started confiding in me. Where else could he turn? For your sister, he was just too different. She's never had a worry in her life. But I know what it's like to be persecuted. Yes, I gave the boy my IBM stock. He should take it, I told him, and run away as fast as he could."

"But Grams, I don't think Dad and Mom think that's the right thing to do."

"Your parents," said Grams, shrugging, "what do they know? Run home, Teddy, and tell them to stop all the fuss." I rose to leave, but I was still shaking.

"Go on now," she said. "And don't be such a stranger." I reached for Grams and hugged her hard.

As soon as I was out the door, I knew where to look. I headed for the bus depot, praying I'd get there in time. Sure enough, Jonathan was hovering behind the newsstand, waiting for the next bus. When he saw me coming, his eyes widened with surprise. He waved me over. I was so out of breath when I caught up with him that I could barely speak.

"Easy there, Teddy. What are you doing here?" A small tattered suitcase stood at his feet; a bulging knapsack was strapped on his back.

"I've been all over town looking for you," I sputtered. "My dad's called the police. He wants the certificates back. They're not really yours."

"Sophie gave them to me," he said sheepishly. "I tried not to take them, but she's been fussing at me about it for weeks. Then last night my uncle really went bananas, and I knew I had to make a move."

At that moment the bus turned the corner with a police car right on its tail. The siren pierced the air.

"As soon as the bus stops, hurry up and get on," I told Jonathan. "I know just how to divert their attention."

He pulled the stocks out of his coat pocket and shoved them in my hands. "You're right, Teddy. I have to do this on my own. Give these back to Sophie. Tell her thanks and I'll never forget her. And say good-bye to Glory for me. I'm sorry I made her so mad."

When the bus screeched to a halt, Jonathan jumped on and I rushed around to the other end, bumping right into the policeman. "He went that-a-way." I pointed toward the station. "Over there. Look!"

"Hold on, sonny boy," the cop said, grabbing my arm. "What are you up to here?" I guess policemen and bulldogs don't have the same reactions. I started babbling a mile a minute trying to stall him until the bus finally pulled away. Then I handed the certificates over to him. He thought I was Jonathan and hauled me off to the station.

My dad had to come and bail me out. Once he discovered Grams' precious IBM stock was back safe and sound, he decided not to press charges. My family thought I was a big hero for getting it back. Maybe I am, but for a different reason. The real hero is Jonathan, but only Grams and I know it. Every now and then, I take out his lucky coin and think about him, wonder where he is, what he's doing. I like to imagine him high in the mountains, sitting in front of a fire in his log cabin. Who knows? Maybe one of these days I'll turn around and there he'll be, coming my way at some unexpected moment. I hope I'm right in the middle of hitting a home run.

ABOUT THIS STORY

While walking her dog—an English bulldog named Jasper, by the way—Jan Greenberg noticed a group of young people playing baseball. One boy didn't seem to be a very good player, and he finally gave up and wandered off with a discouraged look on his face. "As a child, I was often the last to be chosen for a team, so I knew exactly how he felt," says Greenberg. "I began to think 'What if . . . ?' which is often the way stories begin for me." The grandmother in the story was inspired by Ms. Greenberg's mother-in-law, who was famous in St. Louis for her wonderful hats. Jonathan Briggs, the author says, "is based on a boy I once knew in high school. Our house was a safe haven for him, and, like Teddy, I wonder whatever happened to him."

ABOUT THE AUTHOR

Putting a lot of her own experiences and feelings into her books for young people, Jan Greenberg has written a number of novels that deal with characters who face problems. In *A Season In-Between*, for example, a thirteen-year-old girl has to deal with the illness and death of her father. And in *No Dragons to Slay*, a high school athlete has to contend with his own illness and possible death. Ms. Greenberg's work is not all serious, however, as any reader can see in *The Pig-Out Blues* and *Just the Two of Us*. In addition to writing fiction, Ms. Greenberg, with her husband, opened an art gallery in St. Louis that has featured young American artists and musicians. Her interest in art has recently led her to write two nonfiction books about art for young people: *The Painter's Eye: Learning to Look at Contemporary American Art* and *The Sculptor's Eye: Looking at Contemporary American Art*. In these colorful and informative books, young people are encouraged to talk about art and to look at it from a fresh perspective.

ABOUT THE EDITOR

Donald Gallo has compiled and edited several collections of short stories for young adults, along with a collection of plays entitled *Center Stage: One-Act Plays for Teenage Readers and Actors*. As an authority in the field of books for young people, Don Gallo has corresponded and talked with dozens of authors who write for this age group. One of the outgrowths of those contacts is *Speaking for Ourselves: Autobiographical Sketches by Notable Authors of Books for Young Adults*, in which students can find out about the lives of many of their favorite authors. Coming soon is a second volume—*Speaking for Ourselves II*—featuring the autobiographies of many more authors. Dr. Gallo, a former junior high school English teacher, is now a professor of English at Central Connecticut State University. He is the 1992 recipient of the ALAN Award for outstanding contribution to the field of adolescent literature.